Closing the Sea

YEHUDIT KATZIR

Closing the Sea

Translated from the Hebrew
by BARBARA HARSHAV

A HELEN AND KURT WOLFF BOOK
HARCOURT BRACE JOVANOVICH, PUBLISHERS
New York   San Diego   London

To my mother

Translation of *Sogrim et ha-yam*

Translation of Mahler from Deryck Cooke, *Gustav Mahler, An
Introduction to His Music*, Cambridge University Press, 1988.

Lyrics of HEIGH HO, words by Larry Morey, music by Frank
Churchill, © copyright 1940 (renewed) by Bourne Co., all
rights reserved, international copyright secured.

Library of Congress Cataloging-in-Publication Data
Katzir, Judith.
[Sogrim et ha-yam. English]
Closing the Sea / Yehudit Katzir; translated from the Hebrew
by Barbara Harshav.
p.   cm.
Translation of: Sogrim et ha-yam.
"A Helen and Kurt Wolff book."
ISBN 0-15-118200-0
I. Title.
PJ5054.K345S6413 1992
892.4'36—dc20   91-34891
Designed by Lydia D'moch
Printed in the United States of America
First United States edition
A B C D E

Contents

Closing the Sea

Schlaffstunde

Once, when summer vacation stretched over the whole summer and tasted of sand and smelled of grapes and a redhead sun
daubed freckles on your face and, after Sukkot, the wind whistled
into a gang of clouds and we galloped home through the ravine
in a thunderstorm and the rain stabbed your tongue with mint
and pine and the neighborhood dogs set up a racket, barking
like uncles coughing at intermission in a winter concert, and
suddenly spring attacked with cats shrieking and the lemon trees
blossoming and again came a hamsin and the air stood still in
the bus but we got up only for Mrs. Bella Blum from the Post
Office, a dangerous-child-snatcher who comes to us in bed at
night with the wild gray hair of a dangerous-child-snatcher and
narrow glasses on the tip of the sharp-as-a-red-pencil nose of a
dangerous-child-snatcher and who smiles with the cunning flat-
tery of a dangerous-child-snatcher and pokes dry-ice fingers into
our faces, and only if we'd give her all the triangular stamps could
we somehow be saved or if we prayed to God, who disguised
himself as a clown in the Hungarian circus and rocked, balancing

himself on the tightrope under the blue canvas of the tent, in high-heeled shoes and wide red-and-white checked pants and then disguised himself as an elephant, turned his wrinkled behind to us and went off to eat supper.

Once, when the world was all golden through the sparkling Carrera vase in the living room on the credenza, which maybe vanished with all the other furniture as soon as we left the room and we peeked through the keyhole to see if it was still there but maybe it saw us peeking and rushed back and a horrible gang of thieves was hiding out in the garage under the supermarket and only Emil and you could solve the mystery because obviously you were going to be an important detective they'd write books about and I'd be your assistant and we experimented with invisible ink made of onion skins and we heated the note in the candle so the writing would emerge and then we trained ourselves to swallow it so it wouldn't fall into enemy hands and we did other training exercises, in self-defense and in not-revealing-secrets even if they torture you and tie you to a bed and put burning matches under your toenails, and we mixed up poison from dirt and leaves and crushed shells and we kept it in yogurt jars and we drew a skull and crossbones on them and hid them with all our other treasures.

When the summer vacation stretched over the whole summer and the world was all gold and everything was possible and everything was about to happen, and Uncle Alfred was still alive and came for afternoon tea and Grandfather and Grandmother went to rest between two and four and left us endless time, we snuck up the creaky wooden steps behind the house to our little room in the attic which was headquarters and we stood at the window where you could view the whole sea beyond the cemetery and you touched my face with your fingertips and said you loved me.

Now we're gathered here, like sad family members at a departure in an airport, around the departures-board at the entrance, where somebody's written in white chalk, two zero zero, Aaron Green, funeral, and I look at the woman sitting on the stone bench next to you, a round straw hat shading her eyes and ripening her mouth to a grape and the sun polishes two knives of light along her tanned shins and then I go up to the two of you, take off my sunglasses and say quietly, Hello, and you stand up hastily, Meet each other, this is my wife. My cousin. I discern the sparkle of the ring and the white teeth among the shadows and touch her soft hand with long long fingers and say again, Hello. And the undertakers, busy at work like angels in their white shirtsleeves, bearded faces, sweaty, carrying on a stretcher the shriveled body under the dark dusty cloth, the head almost touching the fat black behind of the gravedigger, the legs dangling in front of the open fly of the second one, and a frosty wind blowing inside me, as then, and I seek the memory in your eyes but you lower them to her, take hold of her arm and help her up and my spy's eyes freeze on her rounded belly in the flowered dress and see inside her all your children you buried behind the house, in the grove, in the summer vacation between seventh and eighth grade, when on the first morning, as every year, Grandfather came to pick me up from home in his old black car, with Misha, the office chauffeur, who dressed himself up in my honor in a white visor cap and a huge smile with a gold tooth. Misha put my red suitcase in the trunk and opened the back door for me with a bow and a wink and we went to pick you up from the railroad station near the port. On the way, I stuck my head between him and Grandfather and asked him to tell me again how he played for the king of Yugoslavia and Misha sighed and said, That was a long time ago, but I remember it as if it was yesterday. I was a child then, maybe nine, maybe

ten, and I played the trumpet better than anybody in the whole
school and one day they brought me a blue suit with gold buttons
and a tie and stockings up to my knees and a cap with a visor
and said, Get dressed, and they put me next to a flag and said,
Play, and I played so beautiful and strong and King Pavel came
in and the flag rose to the top of the pole and the trumpet sparkled
like that in the sun and so did the gold buttons, who would have
believed a little Jewish boy like that playing trumpet for the king
and he came to me and stroked my head and asked, What's your
name, and I told him, Misha, and Mama was standing there and
crying so they had to hold her up and Papa said to her, Now
I'm happy we have him, because at first he didn't want me at
all, they went to Austria just for a vacation and when they came
back Mama said, I'm pregnant, and Papa told her, Five is enough,
get an abortion, but Mama was very stubborn, like Albert Einstein's mother, his father didn't want him either, and then he
was terrible in school and the teachers called the father and the
father said to him, Albert, you're seventeen years old now, not
a child, what will become of you, but when he was twenty-six
he met Lenin and Churchill and showed them the theory of
relativity and there were a lot of discussions, and he became
famous all over the world, so when I hear about abortions I say,
Who knows what can come out of that child, why kill a human
being. Misha sighed again and lit a cigarette. In the distance you
could already see the big clock over the railroad station. At five
to nine we arrived. Grandfather and I went down to the platform
and Misha waited in the car. Two porters in gray caps were
leaning on their rusty carts, looked at one another from time to
time with half-closed eyes and smoked stinky cigarettes from
yellow packs with a picture of black horses. I was so excited I
had to pee and I hopped around from one foot to the other. At
nine o'clock on the dot we heard a long happy whistle of the

locomotive pulling five rumbling cars. The porters woke up, stomped on their cigarettes with huge shoes and started running back and forth along the platform shouting, Suitcases, suitcases. Terrified, I looked for your face among the hundreds of faces, crushed and scared, against the glass of the windows. Then the doors opened with a hiss and you came down, the very first one, wearing the short jeans all the kids had and a green shirt with emblems on the pockets that only a few had and a checked detective hat they had brought you from England and no other kid had, and you stood there like that next to your father's black suitcase, and looked around with eyes scrunched up like two green slits under your disheveled fair curls, and once again I felt the pain between my throat and my stomach that clutched my breath every time I saw you and even when I thought about you, and I shouted, Here Uli, here Uli, and I ran to you, and then you saw me and smiled and we embraced, and Grandfather came too, and tapped you on the shoulder and said, How you've grown Saul, and he didn't take your suitcase because you were already thirteen and a half and stronger than he, and you put it in the trunk, next to my red one. And Misha took us to Grandfather's office on Herzl Street, whose walls were covered with big shiny pictures with lots of blue, pictures of beautiful places in Israel, the Kinneret and the Dead Sea and Rosh Ha-Nikra and Elat, where there were rest homes, and the government paid him to send Holocaust survivors there, and I always imagined how they arrived there by train, wearing funny coats and hats with sad yellow faces underneath them as in the pictures they showed us in school on the day commemorating the Holocaust-and-Heroism, and they line up there in a long row with all their suitcases tied with rope, and everybody enters in a line and takes off his coat and hat and gets bright-colored clothes and an orange pointy cap, and they sit in chaise longues in the sun and swim

in the sea and eat a lot and convalesce and after a week grow
fat and tanned and smiling like the people in the advertisements
and then they're sent home because new survivors came on the
train and are already waiting in line. Until once, on Saturday,
we went with Grandfather and Grandmother and Misha to visit
one of those rest homes, called Rosh Ha-Nikra Recreation Vil-
lage, and there was no line of survivors at the entrance, and
there was no way to know who was a Holocaust survivor and
who was just a normal person because they all had fat, droopy
pot-bellies and nobody looked especially sad, they were all swimming in the pool and gobbling sandwiches and guzzling juice and
talking loud and playing bingo. So we made up a system to check
who was a real survivor, but I didn't have the courage, I just
watched from a distance as you passed among the chaise longues
on the lawn next to the pool and whispered into everybody's
ear, Hitler, and I saw that most of the people didn't do anything,
just opened their eyes wide in a strange kind of look, as if they
were waking up from some dream and hadn't had time yet to
remember where they were and they closed their eyes right away
and went on sleeping and only one man, big and fat with a lot
of black hair on his chest and on his back like a huge gorilla,
got up and chased you all over the lawn huffing and puffing, his
eyes red and huge, and finally he caught you and slapped you
and shook your shoulders hard and barked, *Paskutstve holerye,
paskutstve holerye*, and you came back to me with red ears, and
you didn't cry and you said it didn't really hurt, but from then
on, every time they mentioned Hitler, in school or on television,
I would think of the gorilla from the rest home instead of the
real Hitler with the little mustache and dangling forelock.

     In the afternoon we went down, as always on the first day
of vacation, to eat in the Balfour Cellar, and the tall thin waiter,
who looked like a professor, and Grandfather told us that many

years ago he really had been a professor in Berlin, wearing glasses in a silver frame and a beard the same color and a black bowtie, gave a little bow because he knew us, and especially Grandfather, who was a regular customer, and pulled out the chairs for us to sit down, and quickly put menus in front of us and said, What will you have, Herr Green, even though Grandfather always ordered the same thing, roast with puree of potatoes and sauerkraut, and a bunch of purple grapes for dessert, and the regular customers around the tables knew us and smiled and waved at us with white napkins, and as I ate I watched the two plywood cooks hung on the wall in their high chef-hats and long aprons and black mustaches curving upward like two more smiles on their mouths, and they looked back at me leaning on half a wooden barrel sticking out of the wall and full, I was sure, of very very good sauerkraut. And once you told me that the restaurant had a secret cellar right underneath us and that was why it was called the Balfour Cellar, and in the cellar there were lots more barrels like those and all of them were full of sauerkraut that could last a long time in case of another Holocaust, and then the limping newspaper-seller came in wearing a dirty gray undershirt soaked with sweat and yelled, Paper get your paper, until the whole restaurant was filled with his sour breath, and Grandfather beckoned to him, and he came to our table and gave him the paper with a black hand, and Grandfather paid him twenty cents even though right next door to the restaurant there was a clean kiosk that had papers and soda and ice-cream-on-a-stick. Then we went back home on the steep road that went by the gold dome and you could see the whole bay from there, and on the way we fooled around on the back seat and played pinch-me-punch-me and boxed and yelled and called each other names, and Grandfather suddenly turned around and said quietly and earnestly, Don't fight, children, human beings have

to love and pity one another, for in the end we all die. And we
didn't understand what he meant but we stopped, and Misha
winked at us in the mirror, and told about Louis Armstrong,
who was the greatest trumpet player and had the deepest lungs,
and when Betty Grable who had the prettiest legs in Hollywood
got cancer he came with his whole orchestra to play for her on
the hospital lawn under her window. Then we got to the house,
and Grandmother opened the door, her tight hairdo rolled in a
braid around her scalp, and pecked each of us on the cheek and
said, Now Schlaffstunde, which always sounded to me like the
name of a cake like Schwartzwalder Kirschtorte or Sachertorte
or Apfelstrudel, which she would bake because they reminded
her of her home overseas, and the steamy fragrant café when
outside it was cold and snowing, but Dr. Schmidt didn't allow
her to eat them because she had high blood sugar which is very
dangerous for the heart. So she only served it to us and Uncle
Alfred and Grandfather, who always said politely, No thank you,
and refused to taste a single bite even though he was very healthy.
But sometimes, when he went to walk Uncle Alfred to the gate,
Grandmother would cut herself a small slice and eat it with quick
bites, bent over her plate, and Grandfather would come back,
stand in the door and observe her back with a tender look, and
wait until she was finished, and only then would he come into
the living room and sit down with the newspaper, pretending
he hadn't seen. They went to their room, and we went out to
the grove behind the house and stretched a strong rope between
two pine trees and tried to balance on it like that clown we once
saw when we were little and Grandfather took us to the Hungarian circus in Paris Square, where there were purebred horses
and panthers with yellow eyes and trained elephants and a beautiful acrobat with long blond hair and the face of an angel who

danced on the tightrope with a golden parasol in her hand, and we decided we'd run away and join that circus after we were trained, but now we only managed to creep along on the rope, and you explained to me that it's important to know in case you have to cross over water. Then we climbed up to our espionage headquarters under the roof, which sometimes was Anne Frank's hiding-place, where we'd huddle together trembling under the table and munch on potato peels and call each other Anne and Peter and hear the voices of German soldiers outside and drop onto the green velvet sofa which Grandmother brought with her when she came to Israel in the ship, and when one of the two wooden headrests collapsed they bought a new sofa for the living room and brought this one here, because it's a shame to throw out a good piece of furniture, and suddenly you said in a pensive voice, Interesting what you feel after you die, and I said, After you die you don't feel anything, and we tried to close our eyes tight and block our ears and hold our breath to feel dead, but it didn't work because even with our eyes closed we could see colors and you said, Maybe by the time we get old they'll invent some medicine against death, and I said, Maybe you'll be a scientist and invent it yourself and you'll be famous like Albert Einstein. Then we played writing words with our finger on each other's back and whispering them. First we wrote the names of flowers, narcissus and anemone and cyclamen, and names of animals, panther and hippopotamus, and names of people we knew, but after a while you said that was boring, and it was hard to guess because of our shirts, so I took off my shirt and lay down on the sofa, my face in the smell of dust and perfume and cigarette smoke that lingered in the upholstery from days gone by, and I felt how your nice finger slowly wrote words we never dared to say, first a-s-s and then, t-i-t and finally w-h-o-r-e, and while I whispered the words in a soft voice between the cushions of the sofa I felt my face burning and my nipples which had just started to sprout hardening against the velvet.

In the afternoon Grandfather and Grandmother came out of the bedroom with pink cheeks, twenty years younger, and at five o'clock on the dot Uncle Alfred came and we never understood exactly how he was related to us, maybe he was one of Grandmother's distant cousins, and her mouth grew thin as a thread whenever his name was mentioned and Grandfather would roar with rage, Bastard, and we didn't know why they didn't like him, whether it was because he was poor or because he once tried to be an opera singer in Paris or some other reason we couldn't guess, and why they entertained him so nicely in spite of it, and Grandmother served him tea and cake, which he would drink and eat and smack his thick red lips and tell again, his eyes melting with regret, about how he was a student in the Paris Conservatoire and lived in a teeny-tiny attic without a shower and without a toilet in Place de la République, and ate half a baguette-with-butter a day, but at seven in the evening he would put on his only good suit and a bowtie and sprinkle eau-de-cologne on his cheeks and go to the opera, where he would stand under a decorated lighted vault and steal the occasional notes that slipped out through the lattices and caressed the statues of the muses and the cornices of the angels, and in the intermission he would mingle with the audience and go inside, because then they didn't check tickets, and find himself an empty seat in one of the balconies, and so with sobbing heart and damp as a clutched handkerchief he saw the last acts of the most famous operas in the world. And here he would usually stand up, sway like a jack-in-the-box, clasp the back of the armchair with his plump fingers, and burst into an aria from Rigoletto or La Traviata or The Marriage of Figaro, and his voice was frail and fragrant and sweet like the tea he had just drunk, and only at the end did it squeak and break like glass, and Grandmother's thin hands smacked one another in dry applause and Grandfather lowered his eyes to the squares of the carpet and muttered, Bravo, bravo, and we didn't know why Uncle Alfred was thrown out of the Conservatoire one day and didn't become a great singer in the Paris opera, and Grandmother wouldn't tell us, she only clenched her mouth even tighter, as if a huge frog would leap out if she opened it. And Uncle Alfred would sit down and sigh and wipe his reddish nose like a strawberry with a wrinkled handkerchief he pulled out of the left pocket of his jacket, and he would hold out his arms to invite us to ride on both sides of the chair, and hug our waists and tell about the cafés of Montparnasse and Montmartre, which was a meeting place for writers and artists and students, and from his mouth strange names flowed with a wonderful sound I'd never heard before anywhere, like Sartre and Simone de Beauvoir and Cocteau and Satie and Picasso, and then he'd caress your hair and say, You'll be an artist too someday, and stroke your back and say, Or a writer, and press his little white hand on your leg with the short jeans and say, Or a musician, and go on strumming with his fingers on your smooth bare thigh as if he were playing a piano, and he didn't say anything to me. He couldn't know that someday, on a steamy shuddering mid-summer afternoon, we'd be standing in the old cemetery at Carmel Beach, our shamed backs to his tombstone, on which were the words, in gold letters as he requested, of the Chinese poet from Mahler's Lied von der Erde:

> When sorrow draws near,
> The gardens of the soul lie wasted,
> Joy and song wither and die,
> Dark is life and so is death.

Now it is time, companions!
Drain your golden goblets to the dregs.

Our backs to his tombstone and our faces to Grandfather wrapped
in a sheet, he hurrying to slip into an eternal Schlaffstunde next
to Grandmother, who died in the winter many years before, but
they didn't take us to the funeral because they didn't want us
to catch cold and miss school, and our faces to the cantor,
whose closed eyes were turned to the sky as he trilled his *El male
rakhamim shokhen bamromim*, and to your father who had turned
completely gray, muttering *Yitgadal v'yitkadash sh'me raba*, and
to my mother hiding her face in her hands, ripping her shirt,
and to the old people responding Amen, their familiar faces
mocking me under their wrinkled masks, waving at me sometimes
and smiling around the tables in the Balfour Cellar which isn't
there anymore, and sometimes dozing off in the chaise longues
of the rest home which was closed years ago, and here's Misha,
who almost didn't get old but without the visor hat and the smile
with the gold tooth, and he's wearing a black kippa and noisily
wiping his nose, and my gaze is drawn to the shriveled sharp face
of a stooped little old woman which is stamped on my memory
as if it had accompanied me throughout my childhood, though
I can't remember where, and I turn to you and seek in your eyes
which don't look straight at me, in your worn-out face, in the
white threads in your hair, desire in me a sharp wild pain like
the whistle of the train now galloping along the shore on its way
to the new station at Bat-Galim, but only tatters of memories
are pulled from me, connecting to one another with their tails
like the colored handkerchiefs from the box of the magician in
the Hungarian circus, and about a week after vacation started
you didn't want to join the circus or practice balancing on the
tightrope between the pines and you didn't want to play Anne

Frank or Emil and the Detectives, you didn't want to play anything with me, you just sat under the big pine tree all day long
and read little books with crinkled bindings and you looked
worried and sad and full of secret thoughts under your checked
cap. At first I tried not to disturb you even though I was insulted,
but by the third day I had had enough. I waited until afternoon
and when Grandfather and Grandmother went for their Schlaffstunde, I crept up behind you, grabbed the book named The
Confession of the Commander's Lover with a picture on the
cover of a soldier in a brown uniform with black boots up to his
knees aiming a huge pistol at a blonde sprawling in the snow
between his legs and wearing only panties and a bra. I hid the
book, and said I wouldn't give it back until you told me what
was going on. You looked at me strangely through your long
light lashes and said, Swear on the black grave of Hitler that
you won't tell anyone in the world ever. I swear, I whispered
solemnly, and to myself I imagined a deep black hole where the
big hairy Hitler of the rest home was standing. Then you told
me that recently, ever since you started reading those books, it
swelled up in your pants and became so hard you had to rub it
with your hand until a kind of white liquid sprayed out of it and
that was the most wonderful feeling you ever had in your life,
like the explosion of a shooting star, but afterward you were
worried because in school they explained to you that women get
pregnant from it, and when you wash your hands it goes into
the pipes of the sewer along with the water and flows into the
sea and a lot of women swim in the sea and it could get into
them under their bathing suits, and not all of it would go into
the sink either because among millions of little seeds some twenty
or thirty were bound to be left on your hand, and sometimes you
had to go on the bus afterward or to basketball or scouts, and it
could get on the money you paid the driver, and from the driver's

hands to the tickets he gives the girls and women of all ages, and then they go back home and go to the bathroom and tear toilet paper and wipe themselves and it gets inside them and they don't even know, and now thousands of women are walking around the streets with babies from you in their swollen bellies, and not only here in Israel, because the sperm can be washed away in the water and even go as far as Europe. An ashamed spark of pride glimmered in your eyes for a moment and died out. I sat silently awhile and thought, chewing on dry pine needles. That was a really serious problem. Meantime you were tossing pine cones, trying to hit the treetrunk opposite, thunk, thunk, thunk. Suddenly I had an idea. I stood up and ran to the kitchen, opened the drawer next to the sink which had all kinds of things you need in a house, matches and bandaids and rubber bands, and took out a few plastic sandwich bags Grandmother used to pack food for the road when we went on a visit Saturday to one of the rest homes, and I ran back and gave it to you and said, Here, do it in this and bury it in the ground. From that day on, the worry and the pride disappeared from your face and we were friends again and played all the old games, and only sometimes did you suddenly stop and give me long pensive looks, and at night I'd creep into the kitchen and count the bags to know how many were missing, and I'd go out barefoot to the fragrant dark grove with gloomy treetops and the sound of rustling and chirping and howling and mysterious hissing, and I'd find the places where dry pine needles were piled up and the earth was loose, and I'd dig with feverish curious hands and panic and bring up the plastic bags from their graves and look at the wonderful liquid in the moonlight for a long time. One day you added the crinkled little books to our treasure and said, I don't need this garbage anymore, I can invent better stories myself, and I said, You'll surely be a writer someday, and I remembered that

Uncle Alfred had said it before me. So we tore the pages out of the books and sat down to cut out the words, especially the coarsest ones, and pasted them into scary anonymous threatening letters to the gang of criminals under the supermarket and to Mrs. Bella Blum of the Post Office, and we gorged ourselves on the chocolate we had stolen earlier from Grandmother's kitchen, where she kept it for baking her cakes, and it tasted a little like almond paste, and suddenly you touched my face with your fingertips, as if to wipe off a chocolate mustache, and you went behind me and wrote slowly on my back, word after word, I-love-you, and hugged me tight. You lay on the sofa, and I lay down on top of you, my face in the soft shadow between your shoulder and your neck, a smell of paste and starch from your green shirt, and your damp fingers stroked the back of my neck for a long time, trembled, hovered over my hair. Stuck together without moving, almost without breathing, only our hearts galloping like horses in a mad race, and I slowly stroked your face, as if I were sculpting it anew, your fair curls and your smooth brow and your eyelids and underneath them is a whole world and your little nose that a finger could slide down like a ski to your lips, where a hot draft breathes on my frozen finger, and you pull up my shirt, your cool hand on my back down and up, then up and down to that nice place where if we were cats our tails would grow out of, and I put my mouth on your mouth, taste the stolen chocolate, our tongues meet, circle, and push each other like two panicky wrestlers, and I tug the shirt up off your smooth chest and my shirt up off my breasts, to press my nipples hard from the cold against the warm soft skin of your panting belly, and I feel a sweetness between my legs as if honey had spilled and a little of it drops on my panties, and that makes me open them and move back and forth on your thigh, and you hug me tight and suck my lips like lemon drops and you put my hand on the hard bulge in your shorts and your face becomes serious and fragile so in it I can see what no one before me has ever seen, and I breathe fast-fast like a little animal without memories, my melted belly stuck to yours the sweetness in my panties more and more until it hurts until I can't and suddenly those spasms inside me the first time so strong and sharp and long and then shorter and faster like flutterings but I don't shout so they won't wake up and I want it never to end but finally it does end and I fall on you breathless as if I had run the sixty-yard-dash, and I see that you too are half fainted, struggling to swallow air, your face burning, and I get off you and lie beside you and discover a big spot on your pants and, excited, I inhale the sharp smell rising from the two of us, a smell not like any other.

Then you looked at me with flashing green eyes and you smiled and kissed me on my cheek, and you wildly pushed aside the hair stuck to your brow and sat up and took off your shirt in one movement and said, Take off yours too. And I took off mine, and you laid your head on my stomach, and we rested like that awhile, my hand stirring your damp hair, and fingers of sun pierced the chinks in the shutter and spread golden fans on the walls. Then I stroked your back and said your skin was soft as velvet, and you said mine was soft as water, and you kissed my stomach and drew strange forms on it with your lips, and you said, When you lie on your back your breasts are as flat as mine, and you licked my nipples, and your tongue was a little rough like a cat's, and you licked and licked until they got hard as cherry pits, and again I felt sweet and smooth between my legs and I wanted it to go on as before, but Grandmother's voice rose from downstairs, sharp and probing, like the periscope of a submarine, Children, where are you, five o'clock tea and cake. We put on our shirts fast and came down and you went to change your pants, while I looked in the gilded mirror in the vestibule. My eyes sparkled like cups of sky, and the whole world, the furniture in the living room and Grandfather and Grandmother and Uncle Albert looked far away and unreal but sharp and clear, as on a stage.

That night I couldn't sleep because I missed you too much, you were sleeping quietly in the room at the end of the hall and maybe your body was dreaming of me. I wanted so much to come to you in the dark and hug you and hear you breathing, but Grandmother was always strict about you sleeping in your father's old room and me in my mother's room, next to their room, so I controlled myself and thought about tomorrow, about the ceremony we planned down to the smallest detail after dinner, when Uncle Alfred had gone and Grandfather and Grandmother sat down in the living room to watch the Friday night news on television, and we whispered back and forth in the kitchen, and we could hear Menachem Begin the new Prime Minister giving a speech about Auschwitz and the Six Million, and then he announced he was willing to meet in Jerusalem with President Sadat, and Grandfather said, At last that idiot came out with something good, and Grandmother called us, You should see this, important news, but we knew that tomorrow's ceremony was much more important, and especially what would come afterward, and there was no way I could stop the film that kept repeating over and over on the dark screen, the film we starred in. And suddenly, from their room, I heard Grandmother scream in a whisper, Aaron, Aaron, and Grandfather woke up and said gently, Yes, Minna, and Grandmother said she couldn't fall asleep, and she told him quietly, but I could hear every word, that in the morning, as she was walking around in the supermarket with the cart to buy food for the Sabbath, she suddenly felt that her mother was standing next to her, in a black fur coat, the one she wore years ago when they said goodbye at the railroad station, and her face was as pale and terrified as it was then, and she told her something, but Grandmother didn't pay attention because she said to herself, It's summer now, why is Mother wearing a fur coat, and before she could understand, her mother wasn't there anymore. I've been calm ever since, Grandmother went on in a harsh whisper, I'm sure it's something very bad. From her face I know something awful is going to happen. Grandfather didn't say anything, he just sang her something very quiet, a tune of yearning without words, and repeated it over and over until it filled me completely, until I fell asleep.

The next day was the Sabbath. Grandfather and Grandmother woke us early to go with them to visit the rest home in Tiberias, and were surprised when we muttered from under the covers that we were tired and wanted to stay home, but they gave in. I remembered what I had heard at night from their room, and I thought to myself, How can ghosts wander around in our supermarket, and why didn't Grandfather comfort her and tell her it was all her imagination and nothing bad would happen, and suddenly I thought, Maybe that whole conversation didn't happen and I only dreamed it, and I decided not to tell anybody, not even you. Grandmother made hard-boiled egg sandwiches for our lunch, and prepared food to take on the road, and my heart began to pound when I heard the drawer next to the sink open and Grandmother whisper to herself, Funny, I remember there was a whole package here. Finally she wrapped it in waxpaper because Misha was already honking for them outside, and pecked each of us on the cheek and said, We'll be back by seven-thirty tonight, behave yourselves, and they left. As soon as the hum of the motor disappeared around the corner, we leaped out of bed and met in the hall, and we started to do everything exactly according to the plan we concocted last night down to the last detail. First each of us took a long and thorough bath, shampooing our hair and cleaning our ears. Then we wrapped ourselves in our sheets, which we tied at the shoulder like Greek togas, and I put on perfume from all the bottles I found on Grandmother's dressing table, and I smeared my lips and cheeks with a lot of red, and my eyes with blue. Then we cut off the tops of the pink flowers Grandmother had bought for the Sabbath, in the golden vase on the credenza, and we plaited two wreaths for our heads. Then we went into the kitchen but didn't eat breakfast because we couldn't swallow a thing, but from Grandmother's hiding-place for candles, next to the hiding-place for chocolate, we stole six Yahrzeit candles, she always kept it full of them because there was always a Yahrzeit for somebody in her family who had remained over there, and from the sewing box covered with flowered cloth we took a pair of scissors, and from Grandfather's linen drawer we took a white handkerchief, and from the pantry a glass of wine, and from the library a small Bible your father got as a Bar-Mitzvah present from his school, and barefoot we went up to our room in the attic with all those things. Then we closed the shutter on the day and on the cemetery and we made it absolutely dark, and we lit the Yahrzeit candles and put them about the room, which was filled with the shadows of scary demons dancing on the ceiling and the walls, and we left one candle on the table, and we put the Bible next to it, and you asked, You ready, and I whispered, Yes, and my heart was pounding, and we stood facing each other, and we put one hand on the Bible and we raised the other with thumb and pinkie together as in the scouts' oath, and I looked straight into your eyes where the flames of the candles were burning and repeated after you slowly, solemnly:

I swear by God and by the black grave of Hitler,
I swear by God and by the black grave of Hitler,
I will never marry another woman,
I will never marry another man,
And I will love only you forever,
And I will love only you forever.

Then we hugged each other and almost couldn't breathe because we knew that that oath was strong as death and to make it even stronger we cut the words out of the Bible and pasted them on a sheet of paper in the light of the candle. The two Gods we found right away in the creation, and woman in the story of Adam and Eve, and grave in the part about the cave of Machpelah. Then we found man and swear and I and of and you and another and love and the and black and will and never. The rest of the words, Hitler and marry and forever, we couldn't find, so we pasted them together from separate letters. When it was all ready, you wrapped the glass in the handkerchief, put it on the floor and stamped on it hard with your bare foot. The glass broke and a big spot of blood spread over the cloth. You dipped your finger in it and signed your name under the oath. Now you, you said. I took a deep breath, picked up a piece of glass, and scratched my big toe hard, from the bottom, so nobody would see the cut, squeezed a drop of blood onto my finger and signed a shaky signature next to your name. Then we wrote the date, the regular date and the Hebrew date, and the exact address, Presidents' Boulevard, Mount Carmel, Haifa, Israel, Middle East, Continent of Asia, Earth, Solar System, Galaxy, Cosmos. Now we'll tear the oath in two and each of us will keep the half with the other's signature, I said what we had planned to do, and you were silent for a moment and suddenly you said, No, let's wrap it up and bury it under the big pine tree, someplace where we can always find it. I thought to myself that we were forbidden to change the plan, but I didn't say anything. We folded the paper in the aluminum foil of yesterday's chocolate and put it in an empty matchbox, which we wrapped with more paper and in a plastic bag you had left over from the ones you stole from the drawer, and we went downstairs. We dug a deep pit with our hands next to the trunk and hid our package, more important to us than anything in the world, but when we covered it with earth and tamped it down with our feet and piled pine needles on it, I became very sad all of a sudden, and I didn't know why.

When we got back to the room, the Yahrzeit candles were still burning and the demons kept jumping wildly on the walls. I knew what was about to happen but I wasn't scared. I thought about Anne Frank and how the Germans caught her before she really had a chance to love her Peter, when she was exactly my age, and I said to myself, I will have a chance. We took off the wreaths and the Greek togas and we spread one sheet on the sofa underneath us, and we lay down, and covered ourselves with the other one, and I caressed your whole body which was warm and breathing fast, and I walked my tongue among hills of light and soft shadows and paths of soap and sweat under the sheet, and suddenly you were over me on all fours and looking at me with sparkling yellow eyes and a savage smile, and I wanted that to happen, and I whispered, Come, and you asked, Does it hurt, and I said, No, and I could hear your heart drumming on my breasts rhythmically I-love-you-I-love-you, and I was filled with tremendous pride.

Then heavy steps grated on the stairs and I whispered, The Germans, and I started trembling, and we held each other tight and clung to the wall, and the door opened, and in the opening in a halo of light stood Uncle Alfred. They apparently forgot to

tell him they were going away and that he shouldn't come today
for tea. He looked at our sweaty bodies and the handkerchief
spotted with blood and the pink flowers scattered over the floor
and the Yahrzeit candles, and he rubbed his strawberry nose in
embarrassment, and his eyes were fixed on some point on your
stomach, maybe your belly button, as he stammered, What's this
children, it's forbidden, at your age, you shouldn't, if Grandmother finds out. We covered ourselves with the sheet and looked
at him cautiously and silently like cats. He lowered his eyes to
the shiny tips of his shoes and went on, Of course I'll have to
tell her, who would have thought, children, cousins, and God
Forbid there'll be a baby with six fingers on each hand, or two
heads, or a little tail like a pig, this is very dangerous, who would
have thought. And he wagged his head from the right shoe-tip
to the left shoe-tip, as if he were setting up a shiny-shoe contest.
Then he looked at you again, and said with no stammering now
that he was willing not to tell anybody on condition that you
agreed to meet him here, tomorrow afternoon, so he could talk
to you and explain what a serious thing it was we had done.
Why only him, I burst out to defend you, and Uncle Alfred said
he regarded you as responsible and that with your sense and
talent he hadn't expected anything like this from you. I agree,
you said quietly, and he left. As soon as the door closed behind
him we jumped off the couch, stood at the window again, with
one hand on the Bible and the other in the air, with thumb and
pinkie together, and I repeated after you the oath we composed
on the spot:

> And even if we have a baby
> With six fingers on each hand
> Or two heads
> Or a little tail like a pig

We will love it as if it was a completely normal baby
With five fingers and one head
And no tail at all.

Then we dressed and cleaned up everything fast before Grandfather and Grandmother got back home. Except the dark red
spot, blossoming on the green velvet, that we left as a souvenir.
Before I fell asleep, I could hear Grandmother whispering into
the golden vase on the sideboard, Funny, I remember buying
flowers for the Sabbath, and Grandfather comforting her gently,
Well, my memory's not what it used to be either, how could I
forget to tell Alfred not to come today for tea.

In the middle of the night I felt horribly nauseous, ran to
the bathroom and stuck my finger down my throat and suddenly
I felt I was throwing up sand, enormous amounts of wet sand,
it filled my mouth and gritted between my teeth, and I spat and
threw up, threw up and spat, and then something else was vom-
ited up from me with the sand, and I looked into the toilet. A
tiny black dog floating stiffly on his side, his legs spread out, his
gums exposed in a creepy smile, watching me with a gaping dead
eye. In horror I slammed down the lid. Outside it was beginning
to turn light.

I wandered around among the trees with my hands in my
pockets, kicking pine cones. You'd been up there for more than
half an hour, closed in the room. What did he have to tell you
that took so much time. I couldn't control myself anymore. I
went up very quietly, opened the door a little, and peered in.
The two of you were sitting on the sofa. With big opera gestures
Uncle Alfred was explaining something to you that I couldn't
hear and from time to time he put his cotton hand on your leg.
Then he wrapped his arm around your shoulders and put his face
which was always flushed, almost purple, close to your face which

was ashen. Suddenly he looked up and saw me. A shadow passed over his eyes. I fled downstairs. I lay under the big pine tree, right over the oath we buried yesterday, and I looked at the green sparkling needles that stabbed the clouds which today were in the shape of a huge white hand. I waited. Time passed, more time, a lot of time passed, and you didn't come down. I remembered the dream I had last night, and I shivered with cold. At last the door opened and Uncle Alfred came out breathing deeply as he went unsteadily down the steps. He buttoned his jacket and rang the front door bell. Grandmother opened the door, said, Hello Alfred, and he went into the house. Then you came running out, you lay down beside me, hid your head against my belly, and muffled your howls of anguish. Your whole body shook. I held you. What happened, what did he tell you, I whispered. We have to kill him, you cried. Your hot tears were absorbed by my shirt. I had never seen you cry like that. But what happened, what did he do, I asked again. We have to kill him we have to kill him, you wailed, your feet kicking the ground. But what did he do, hit you, tell me what he did, I pleaded. You lifted your burning wet face where the tears and the snot were running but you didn't care, and you said quietly, Today I'm going to kill him. I looked into your red eyes, with two black pits in them, and I knew that today Uncle Alfred would die.

Within minutes we had a fatal solution of poison made of shells ground up with two ants, a mashed piece of pine cone, and yellow dog-doo. We mixed it all up with pine tar so the ingredients would stick together. My job was to ask Grandmother if I could make the tea today, and to pour the poison into Uncle Alfred's cup. I chose the big black cup for him so I wouldn't confuse it with another and also because I thought the poison would work better in a black cup. I added five spoons of sugar and stirred it well, trying to hear what they were saying in the living room to make sure he wasn't telling on us in spite of everything. They were talking very quietly and only separate words reached me, Dr. Schmidt, chest X-ray, diagnosis, and Dr. Schmidt again. They were talking about diseases. I calmed down. On the tea cart I also put the special two-layer Schwartzwald-ertorte that Grandmother baked and I didn't understand what it was in honor of, maybe it was his birthday today. As soon as I entered with the tray, they shut up. Uncle Alfred said, Thank you, and a sad smile clouded his face. You came in too, your eyes dry now, and we huddled together in the chair, waiting with awful tension to see him drink and die on the spot. First he greedily polished off three pieces of cake. Then he sipped noisily, smacked his lips, faced us, and declared, Now I will sing you the first Lied from Mahler's Lied von der Erde. He cleared his throat twice, clasped his hands on his stomach, and started singing in German which we couldn't understand. His voice burst out of his chest as a solemn trumpet blast, rose to a great height both bold and trembling like a tightrope walker, and suddenly it fell and plunged into a dark abyss, where it struggled with fate, pleaded, prayed, shouted like a hollow echo, whimpered, abased itself, the face that of a drowning man, tears flowed from his eyes and from Grandmother's eyes too, she understood the words, and even Grandfather blew his nose a few times, and we looked at each other and knew the poison we mixed was also a magic potion, and we held our breath to see him sink into the carpet in the middle of the song, but Uncle Alfred finished it with a long endless shout and his arms waved to the sides and hit the credenza, and the gold vase teetered a moment in surprise and then slid off and smashed on the floor into sparkling slivers. Uncle Alfred sat down, panting heavily, and whispered, Sorry, and Grandmother said, It's nothing, and she came and kissed him on the cheek and Grandfather didn't look at the squares of the carpet and didn't murmur, Bravo, but shook his hand and looked into his eyes and said, Wonderful, wonderful, and Uncle Alfred took another sip of the poisoned tea, and stood up to go, and said to us, Goodbye, and caressed you with his gaze, but we didn't answer, we only looked at him with hatred, and they accompanied him to the door, and wished him good luck, and Grandfather patted him on the shoulder and said, Be strong, Alfred, and Uncle Alfred said hesitantly, Yes, and the door closed behind him and Grandfather and Grandmother looked at each other a moment, and Grandmother nodded her head and brought a broom and dustpan and swept up the slivers.

At night I woke up to the sound of coughing and an awful screeching laughter and I heard Grandmother telling Grandfather in the kitchen, Now I know what she said, now I know what she wanted to tell me then. And the awful laugh was heard again, as if it weren't Grandmother laughing but some demon inside her. I got up to peer from behind the door, and I saw her sitting at the table, her long hair disheveled and in her nightgown and her mouth stained with cherry juice and chocolate, a knife clutched in her fist over the ruins of Alfred's two-layer cake, and Grandfather in pajamas grabbing her wrist and pleading, Enough, enough now, you've already eaten too much, and Grandmother struggled to free her hand and the screeching voice of the demon burst out of her, Just one more little piece, just one more little piece, and Grandfather held her and cried, Don't leave me alone, Minna, please don't leave me alone, I can't make it alone. I ran away from there to your room. Your breathing was heavy, uneven. I got in under your blanket and hugged you and put my head next to yours. The pillow was soaked.

The next day we went with Misha and Grandfather and Grandmother who sat in front, her braid now pinned together, and Misha let them off at Rambam Hospital and took us to the

beach at Bat-Galim, and we took off our clothes and had our
bathing suits on underneath, and Misha looked like a lifeguard
with his visor cap and broad chest, all he needed was a whistle.
He sat down in a chaise longue at the edge of the water, and
you ran into the sea with a spray splashing colorfully and you
plunged into the waves, and I ran in behind you and also plunged
because I wanted to feel what you were feeling, and my eyes
burned and I swallowed salt water, and when I came back to the
shore, you were already standing there and shaking your curls,
and we sat down on the sand next to Misha, leaning against his
sturdy legs, and we watched the sea and were silent because none
of us had anything to say. Then I asked Misha to tell us again
how he played for the king of Yugoslavia because I knew how
much he liked to tell it, and I thought maybe that would save
the situation. He was silent a moment, and suddenly he said
quietly, It wasn't I who played for the king, it was another boy,
he was also called Misha, and he played better than I did, so
they chose him to wear the uniform with gold buttons, and the
trumpet sparkled in the sun, and the flag went up to the top of
the flagpole, it was so beautiful I'll never forget it, and King
Pavel came and patted his head and his mother cried so they
had to hold her up, and I stood there in the line with all the
children and I cried too. He wiped his nose, and then he went
on, as if to himself, But that Misha isn't here anymore, Hitler
took him, all of them, all of them, my parents too, my brothers
and sisters, I'm the only one alive, the sixth child, the one they
didn't want, because Papa and Mama got married very young,
they were cousins, but the family decided to marry them off at
thirteen, that's how it was done in those days, and every year
they had a baby, every year a baby, until Papa said, enough. But
then they went for a vacation in Austria and when they came
back Mama was pregnant again. Misha fell silent and lit a cig-

arette, and then he said out of the blue, Your grandfather is a
fine man, there aren't many people like him. We quietly watched
a young man who finally managed to walk on his hands and a
man who threw a stick in the water and his big dog charged in
barking and swam and brought the stick out in his mouth and
the man patted his head. I took an ice-cream stick and drew a
house and a tree and the sun on the wet sand, and the waves
came and erased my picture. And the sea slowly turned yellow
and we got chilly so we dressed and went to get Grandfather and
Grandmother, who were waiting for us at the entrance to the
hospital with gray faces and looking suddenly very old.

A few days later Grandmother told us that Uncle Alfred had
died in the hospital. She wiped her tears and said, He had a
disease in his lungs and the operation didn't succeed. But we
knew the real reason, and we didn't dare look at each other as
we walked with Grandmother, who was weeping for Alfred and
for herself, and with Grandfather, who was weeping for Grandmother, and with our parents and the other three people we
didn't know, behind the undertakers busy like angels in white
shirtsleeves and sweaty faces, carrying the shriveled body on a
stretcher under a dark dustcloth, the head almost touching the
fat black behind of the first gravedigger, the legs dangling in
front of the open fly of the second one, and I thought, It could
be anyone under the cloth, maybe it's not him, but when we
got to the open grave the cantor said his name and a desperate
crying burst out of me because I knew you couldn't move time
backward. And you stood silently on the other side of the black
grave, and I knew that Uncle Alfred would always be between
us, and after the funeral your father would take you home, long
before the end of summer vacation because Grandmother already
didn't feel well, and in a few months, in the winter, she would
die too, and Grandfather would close the office on Herzl Street

and move to an old people's home, and he would go on talking
to her all those years as if she were still beside him, and we would
never again be together in our little room under the roof, and
only sometimes, before sleep came, you would crouch over me
on all fours and look at me with yellow pupils and I would whisper
to you, Come, and I would feel your heart drumming on my
breasts, until the last flutter. I wipe my tears and go with all the
old people to put a little stone on the grave, and now everyone
is turning to go, but I stay another moment at Uncle Alfred's
yellowed marble, I know you're standing here next to me. Up
close you can see that I too have lines at the corner of my mouth
and many gray hairs, and the two of us read by heart the lines
from the first lied of Das Lied von der Erde, whose words we
didn't understand then, and I put a little stone under the words
and you put a little stone and then you put your hand on my
shoulder and say, Let's go. My mother and your father are walking
in front of us, whispering about the city's plan to destroy the old
house and dig up the grove to build an expensive apartment
building on the site, and I see the ground, which can't still be
holding all we buried there, it will split open and the highrise
will crack and collapse. Misha comes behind us and sighs and
says, If you could only go backward in life, even one minute,
and I know exactly what minute he wants to go back to. And
at the gate stands the stooped-over old woman whose shriveled
face is so familiar, and she grabs my sleeve with a trembling hand
and screeches, Maybe you don't remember me but I remember
your grandfather very well, he was a regular customer of mine,
in the old Post Office. You're Mrs. Bella Blum from the Post
Office, I whisper and my heart turns pale, and for a split-second
I see eyeglasses on the end of a sharp nose, gray hair, icy fingers
reaching out for the necks of children and triangular stamps, and
I remember the anonymous threatening letters, and I glance over

at you, but you're looking at your shoes covered with dust and
you say, I have to go, we have a meeting at the factory, and
once again I touch her soft hand under the purplish straw hat.
Suddenly a strong wind comes from the sea and snatches the hat
off her head and rolls it down the path, and she runs after it
among the tombstones in her fluttering flowery dress, with her
rounded belly, with the strips of her chestnut hair, flinging out
her full arms to catch it, but the hat mocks her, it flies into the
sky like a purple butterfly, and just as it's about to light on the
sharp top of the cypress, it changes its mind, flips over twice and
lands on the tombstone of Abba Hushi the famous mayor of
Haifa, and you and Misha and all the other men volunteer to
get it for her and you jump around among the graves, but the
hat is already far away from there, crushed and ashamed between
Hanoch ben Moshe Gavrieli born in the city of Lodz and Zilla
Frumkin model wife and mother, who lie crowded next to each
other, and all of you are flushed and sweating, but the hat pulls
away again with a splendid somersault and soars, and you chase
it, look up and wave your hands, like survivors on a desert island
to an airplane, then the hat loses its balance and spins around
itself like a dancer with a jumble of purple ribbons and lands
with a bang outside the gate and lies on its side and laughs with
its round mouth, and she runs to it, heavy and gasping and bends
over and picks it up and waves it high in the air and brimming
with joy she turns to you with sparkling eyes, I got it, I got it.

Fellini's Shoes

To David Greenberg, with thanks

1

I was late for work that day even though I left home early enough. It was all because of that old woman chirping behind me, *Meydele, meydele,* on Dizengoff Street at the corner of Jabotinsky as she caught me by the sleeve so I should help her cross the street. I glanced at her and didn't understand why she couldn't cross by herself. She looked all right to me; almost a head shorter than me, but standing straight. Her hair was white except for a few reddish strands on her forehead. Her eyes twinkled, two blue beetles on an orange lawn. Her nose poked out like a parrot's beak between two flushed cheeks, and underneath it a tiny smile was painted with red lipstick. She wore a long brown coat even though it was after Passover and getting warm, and a rakish red kerchief was tied around her neck pirate-style. Her small feet in those old women's orthopedic shoes with holes stepped jauntily across the street as her twisted fingers hooked tightly around my wrist. When we reached the other side, I tried to free my hand and say, Good luck, old woman, be well, but she tightened her grip, said *Dort, dort,* and her free arm, a peeling

patent-leather bag hanging from it, stretched forward, showing
where she wanted to go, and she explained something in excited
Yiddish, hurrying with quick steps and pulling me after her. I
didn't understand a thing. I don't know Yiddish, just a few words.
So I went with her a little farther, but at the corner of Arlozorov
I said, That's it, ma'am, I have to get to work, but she didn't
hear or pretended not to hear, just stretched her arm forward,
pointed to the horizon, between the buildings, and said again,
Dort. I didn't know what to do. My shift began at five, in fifteen
minutes, and I needed time to change and put on makeup; Fedida
yelled if you didn't come exactly on time and with your makeup
perfect. But this old woman really seemed to need help, and I
couldn't just leave her like that. I remembered the awful reports
on television lately about how old people were treated, so I
decided to go with her a little farther; maybe we would get to
where she had to go soon. She examined me with a shrewd look,
smacked her lips with pleasure, like the witch in Hansel and
Gretel, and said, *A shayne maydele.* So we walked, almost ran,
along Dizengoff Street. All of a sudden, near the kiosk on the
corner of Ben-Gurion Boulevard, she stopped and wouldn't
move. Again I tried to free my hand, which was hurting from
her viselike grip, but the old woman thrust her fingers in my
sleeve and started stamping her little feet with the stubbornness
of a spoiled child. What do you want, I asked her, but she didn't
answer. She just stood straight, with her parrot nose and her red
kerchief and her two blue beetles flashing and offended. Maybe
she's thirsty, I said to myself, and bought her a bottle of orange
juice. With a grunt, she sucked the juice through a straw and
put the empty bottle on the counter with a proud thump. Now
let's go, I said and pulled her hand impatiently. By now it was
terribly late, maybe a quarter after five. But my old woman
wouldn't budge. She stuck out a sharp tongue, yellow from the

juice, and licked her lips. She wants me to buy her ice cream too, I thought, furious, she's really going too far, this nervy grandma. I bought two ice-cream bars, vanilla and chocolate, and let her choose. She took the chocolate and finally agreed to go on. Licking her ice cream, she chattered in my ear good-naturedly, bursting into cackles of laughter from time to time. I began to suspect that she actually had no place to go to. Maybe she had escaped from an insane asylum. Suddenly I was frightened. Excuse me, sir, do you know Yiddish, do you speak Yiddish, ma'am, I asked every elderly person who walked by. No one knew Yiddish. Most people didn't even answer. The old woman fell silent and looked sad. By now it was beginning to get dark, and I knew it was almost six. I could make it to the seven-o'clock shift and say I got mixed up with the shifts. But what to do with this strange grandma who had stuck to me for more than an hour now, her whole face smeared with chocolate ice cream? I thought of taking her with me to the hotel and sitting her down in the lobby. But then what? In my little rented room there was hardly enough space for me. Meanwhile, she had discovered some brown spots on her red pirate's kerchief and started weeping silently, wiping her tears and red nose on the sleeve of her coat. But then she heard the sound of water, let go of my hand, and ran up the steps to the fountain in the square. When I got there, I found her scrubbing her kerchief in the fountain. Her peeling patent-leather bag was lying on the bench, so I took the opportunity to look in it for her ID or an envelope with an address, something to tell me where she belonged. I found a lipstick, a small bottle of cologne, a compact with a little mirror, a pink comb, a white handkerchief, an old photograph of a man in a dark suit, his black hair shiny and combed back and his look soft and harsh under thick eyebrows. He resembled Richard Gere, my favorite actor. On the back of the photograph some words were written in a foreign language with a blurred pencil. At the bottom of the bag there were lots of loose coins. At least she has a little money, I thought, but when I took out a few of them and examined them in the light of the streetlamp, I saw that they were worthless, coins from long ago. That was all. No ID, no health-insurance booklet, not even a key. I didn't know what to do. I sat down on the bench and gazed at my old woman, who had finished laundering her kerchief and was waving it over her head, spraying water on herself and everything around her. Then she climbed up on the bench around the fountain, smiled sweetly, and in a high voice sang:

> Ot dort, ot dort, oyf yenem ort,
> Shteyen zikh feygelekh tsvey, oy, tsvey!
> Zey shmuessn zikh, zey kushn zikh,
> Zey kushn zikh, zey lyuben zikh—
> Akh, sara fargenign hobn zey,
> Oy, zey!

She repeated the song again and added a little dance to it, ending with a quick turn and a deep curtsy, accompanied by majestic waves of the red kerchief. Finally she clutched the kerchief to her chest, fluttered her eyelashes, and breathed emotionally, like a leading lady after a successful premiere.

Applause rose from the twilight, from the old men sitting on the benches of the square at dusk, and they gathered around her and asked for an encore. She agreed to sing it again, and again, until I knew the song by heart, but the old men clucked with rapture and called out, Bravo, bravo, bis. The birds, who froze for a moment on the three taut electrical wires like a row of black notes, shook themselves out of their listening and flew off with an excited rush of wings over her head. I took advantage of the audience surrounding her to slip away. One of those old men, I told myself, will understand her chattering and take care of her. Yet it seemed to me that she looked at me accusingly from the heights of her stage of splendor. I felt like a traitor.

2

The guard at the employees' entrance sat in his usual place, in the booth next to the timeclock. On his little black-and-white TV, a basketball game was on, sliced vertically here and there by black lines, but that didn't keep him from staring greedily at the screen as he ate a tuna sandwich left over from the customers' lunch. I said hello to him, and he muttered something with his full greasy mouth. As I stuck my card into the timeclock, which printed 6:43, I thought to myself that the man didn't have a chance of becoming a hotel doorkeeper. Only in his dreams would he see himself standing at the main entrance by the revolving glass door, dressed in a red uniform with gold stripes on the cuffs, a visor cap, and white gloves, opening the doors of American limousines with an elegant flourish. I ran down to the dressing room, smelling the soap fumes that rose from the laundry. I opened my metal locker, put on the awkward yellow uniform, and pinned the plastic tag to my chest, Millie in English, so the customers could call their waitress by her first name and feel at home. Then quickly, at the mirror over the sink, I put on my makeup. A *shayne maydele*, I smiled to myself. It's not often somebody tells me I'm pretty. I have enormous eyes that take up almost my whole face. Toad's eyes, Meir the barman says, laughing at me, eyes like headlights. I put extra makeup on them to make them smaller.

The lobby was unusually busy and full that evening. All the tables were taken and people were standing in the aisles, waiting for a seat. Fedida ran past me, muttering to himself, A madhouse,

a madhouse. The jacket of his mustard uniform was open, his
face flushed, and his black bowtie twisted to one side. With his
little mustache and buckteeth, Pedida always reminded me of
Bugs Bunny. I started working so he wouldn't notice me and
remember that I was supposed to have been there at five. Meir
shoved a tray with twelve glasses of foamy beer into my hands
and said, Table 48. Excuse me, excuse me, I shouted nervously,
trying to get through the jackets and furs whose owners pecked
at each other with sharp red mouths and ignored the heavy tray
I was carrying. When I reached the table, the glasses started
rattling, because five of the men sitting around it were giants,
human mountains, and one of them was black, while the other
seven were dwarfs, adult men the size of eight-year-old children.
All twelve were drunk, joking in loud English and slapping each
other on the shoulder. Their table was filled with half-empty
beer glasses and bowls of olive pits. More olives, more peanuts!
screamed a drunk dwarf in a red cotton shirt. When I returned
to the bar with the bowls, Meir told me that a film crew had
arrived from America, two hundred people, to do a series of
children's stories in Israel, and a famous basketball team from
Houston Texas had come on the same plane. The dwarfs and
the basketball players didn't know each other at all in America,
said Meir, amazed, but on the plane they started drinking together. Those dwarf bastards, every one of them has a normal-
size wife and they have children, he laughed, but guess what,
they brought along three actresses, each one a living doll, and
he shut his eyes and licked his lips with his thick red tongue.

   I was excited. I always get excited when a film crew comes.
I spot the director right away—tall and tan, his silvery white
curls, the confident blue gaze amid tiny laugh lines around his
eyes. He sits at the head of the table wearing a brown leather
jacket and a loose colorful tie; he holds a glass of scotch-on-the-

rocks and speaks with his staff in the quiet tone of a man who knows what he's talking about. Sometimes, to read from the script, he puts on glasses with metal frames, and then his eyes grow soft and he looks as if he needs a hug. I always try to get him to look at me when I put another whiskey down in front of him, carefully, on a round napkin. Then the female star joins him. She always has a strange foreign name, Diana or Joanna, and acts as if she owns the place. Owns the whole world. In the morning, she comes through the lobby in a tiny bikini, on her way from the pool to the dining room. Water drips from her perfect body onto the expensive carpets spread obsequiously under her beautiful legs. In the afternoon, she returns from a day of shooting: her scorched hair circles her face like a wild sun; her cheeks are red, her lips swollen with dryness, and she wets them with her tongue and tosses weary smiles at everyone and no one in particular. At dusk, she appears fresh after a shower and an afternoon nap between cool clean sheets. She's wearing jeans now, and her hair is pulled back. She orders a dry martini, lights the one-cigarette-a-day she allows herself, puts on her glasses, and studies her lines for the next day. Later, she returns with the crew from an evening out or from a terrific dinner. In a black mini, made-up and beaming, she stretches her long legs over the arm of her chair and puts her blond curls on the leading man's shoulder with a bubbly laugh like the champagne she has been drinking. The crew and the silver-haired director compete with each other to make her laugh, and Fedida and Meir stand not far from her, their necks craning and their feet tapping nervously. They are ready to leap into motion at the slightest movement of her hand, to fulfill all her wishes—to bring her Russian caviar or squeeze fresh mango juice for her in the middle of the night.

In the winter, when the film crew leaves and there's practically no work, I lean on the bar, listen to the rain outside and the boring waltzes of the pale piano player, and think about that director. Someday he'll look right into my eyes and then get up and come to me and say quietly, You know, Millie, you have a very interesting face. I want you for my film. And I'll smile at him and take a tray loaded with coffeepots and cups and glasses and cakes, and I'll stand in the middle of the lobby and throw the tray to the floor so all the expensive dishes smash and the drinks spray, making spots on the carpet and the satin and velvet dresses of the rich women who just came from a fashion show. Then I'll go to him and say, OK, I'm coming with you, and Fedida and Meir and all the rest will stand and look at me in amazement and anger, but they won't dare do anything, and they'll even give me their servile waiters' smiles when I leave the lobby forever, arm-in-arm with him.

Afterward, I clear the tables and put the tray with the dirty dishes on the counter, where Fawzi gives me a yellow-toothed smile as he hurries off to put the leftovers in his mouth and the plates in the dishwasher. He knows that Meir will come into the kitchen in a little while to smoke a cigarette after his shift and play Arab Dog with him. In this game, Meir gives Fawzi orders, for example, Arab Dog give me a light, Arab Dog bring me a Coke, Arab Dog say your mother's a dirty Arab whore, and Fawzi has to do everything Meir tells him or he gets hit. Sometimes, when Meir's feeling really mean, he says, Arab Dog go down to the storeroom and bring up some peacock's milk. Fawzi will come back with a frightened face, spread his hands and say, There isn't any, and then Meir will let him have it. Meir likes this game a lot. Fawzi doesn't. Every day, he gives me his yellow smile because he thinks I have influence with Meir. But I can't help; Meir doesn't listen to what I say even though after work we'll drive in his jalopy to some deserted beach and get into the backseat and he'll tell me I'm his girl and fondle my breasts and pull down my panties and put it in and come without even any kissing. Then he'll take me home and on the way promise me again that this week he'll get the key to suite 1601, it's really no problem for him with his connections at the reception desk. Once, when he was working in room service, the clerks let him take a cart with champagne there and he remembers exactly how the suite looks. He describes for me in great detail the night we'll spend there like royalty, with champagne and a Jacuzzi and movies on the video. At my house, he makes me smoke a cigarette with him, even though I don't like that brand, and he repeats, You're my girl. And he leaves and I go to sleep.

At about eight-thirty, they called me to the phone: the hotel owner asked politely if I would bring a smoked salmon sandwich, a glass of orange juice, and a pot of coffee to his office. He always asks for me because I remember to cut his sandwich into quarters. The hotel owner has only one arm, so it's difficult for him to cut the sandwich by himself. His left arm, plastic, comes out of the sleeve of his jacket as pink and smooth as a doll's. I took the elevator to the seventeenth floor, the top floor, knocked on the door and rolled the cart into the splendid office, next to the suite where he lives with his enormous black dog named Znaforts. They spend most of the day in the office; the hotel owner works and Znaforts, blind, lies on the rug at his feet, giving a long heart-wrenching whimper from time to time. At twilight, through the windows of the lobby, I see their black silhouettes against the gilded sea, walking on the beach, the long tall silhouette of the man and the low broad silhouette of the dog. At night, Znaforts is allowed to wander around the hotel. Sometimes, when I'm working the night shift, he passes me panting like a dark ghost. I placed the cut-up sandwich, the glass of juice, and the pot of coffee on the low glass table, where the hotel owner eats his dinner, and waited politely as he took some money from his wallet. It always takes him time because of his arm. I gazed at the Persian rugs, the wooden desk with feet carved like an eagle's talons, and the weights and golden pens on it, the statues of naked women in the muscled arms of creatures who are men on top and billygoats on the bottom, and I looked at the pictures on the wall. There was a new one, which I liked, a picture of a bride and groom flying in the sky with a goat and a violin. I pointed to the picture and said, Enjoy it. Thank you, he said seriously—he never smiles—and gave me a tip, which was big, as usual. I turned to go. Znaforts raised his blind eyes to me, sniffed the air, and whined softly.

When I got back to the lobby, I saw the giants striding grandly toward the elevator, with the seven dwarfs behind them, swaying from side to side, flushed, babbling. I wanted to sing to them, Heigh-ho, heigh-ho, it's off to work we go. The jackets and furs had also gone into the big hall, to a cocktail party in honor of some Member of the Knesset or other important person. No movie director in sight. There were only the regular customers—at table 27 sat Mrs. Brown, manager of the hotel gallery. Everything about her is brown: her hair, eyes, dress, shoes, and the big freckles on the back of her hands, and the long thin cigarette she holds in her brown nicotine-stained fingers. As every evening, she went over the menu thoroughly, then asked in a smoky voice, What do you have today, and after I whispered in her ear all the cakes, ice cream, sandwiches, soft drinks, and hot beverages, she ordered, as always, a pot of boiling water and a cup and made herself camomile tea from a bag she took out of her brown purse.

At table 29, as usual, sat Mr. Gordon, shriveled and shaking in his wheelchair, casting loving glances at the fat smiling black nurse his children in America hired to take care of him when his Parkinson's got worse, and to make the funeral arrangements when he died. But Mr. Gordon prefers his devoted nurse, with her ample bosom and white uniform, to the Holy Land, and he's been living with her now for five years in suite 1602 at the expense of his children's inheritance, and every day they sit in the lobby between five and six in the afternoon and look lovingly at each other, and again after dinner, between eight and ten-thirty, when she puts him to bed. Only on Tuesdays, when the English detective he likes is on television, is he allowed to stay up.

At the bar was Rita, blinking, shifting from one long leg to the other long leg in red high-heeled shoes and sticking out her little round ass in a tight red mini. The security guards, in gray suits and traffic-light ties, their hand radios beeping like kids' walkie-talkies, gave her ravenous looks and intercepted any girl who tried to horn in on Rita's territory and livelihood. On slow nights like tonight, Rita leans her pointy elbows on the bar and tells Meir, sincerely, that what she really wants is a quiet life, a husband and kids and a poodle. Every now and then she blinks her heavy-lashed eyes hard, so it seems that she doesn't mean anything too seriously. Meir smokes a cigarette and listens to her low voice with a philosophical expression, but his little eyes are squinting anxiously at the glass dish where he keeps the maraschino cherries to trim his cocktails, and I also stare hypnotically, at the long-fingered hand with perfect red nails reaching for the dish and choosing a sparkling red cherry, and popping it into her full red mouth which sucks the sweet fruit slowly while her hand goes back and reaches for the dish and another cherry. If his eyes drop into the dish from so much squinting, I think to myself, Rita will take them with her red-fingernailed hand and suck them unwittingly, one eye then the other. Two weeks

ago, on the beach, in the backseat of the car, after he zipped up
his pants and lit a cigarette, Meir told me in confidence that
Rita was once a man. I didn't know whether to believe him;
perhaps he just wanted to get even with her for the cherries.

At table 35, behind the plant, sat a man I didn't know, but
he kept looking at me. He was about sixty. Some of his long
white hair was combed back to hide his bald spot. I went to take
his order. All the wrinkles smiled around his sad brown eyes
when he asked, What's your name, my dear. Millie, I pointed
to my plastic tag, and then I said, But my family calls me Malka,
and I blushed terribly. I don't know what made me say that.
Nobody in the hotel knew my real name, not even Meir. Malka,
Malka, he repeated, as if he were talking about the Queen of
England, since Malka means queen. Then he asked in a fancy
way, Would you honor me with a cup of hot? I didn't understand
what he wanted, so he explained that that was how you asked
for a cup of tea in old Hebrew literature. I fixed him a nice tray
with three slices of lemon on a little plate and a small pitcher
of milk, because I forgot to ask him which he preferred, and I
was careful to put the napkin to the right of the saucer, under
the spoon, as Fedida had trained us, and I made sure the tea was
strong enough. I don't know why I wanted everything to be so
nice and neat for him. Maybe because of the way he talked, or
because of the starched white shirt he was wearing, or the black
shoes that were so shiny they caught the light of the lamp over
him in two stars, one star in each shoe. Just as I was about to
take the tray to the man's table, Fedida appeared, waving in my
face a white paper, the work schedule. Five, it says here five,
not seven, five, he shouted. I tried to explain about the old lady
and how I couldn't leave her alone, but he just glared at me with
eyes like one more pair of buttons above the two rows of polished
buttons on his uniform, and he said, I'll get you thrown out of

this hotel. I poured the tea for table 35 without looking at the
man so he wouldn't see the tears in my eyes, but maybe he saw
them anyway, because he thanked me with a warm soft smile. I
wanted to jump into his smile and curl up in it as in a quilt so
no one could find me. Then he held his hand out and said, Allow
me to introduce myself, Joshua Spielman, film director. I shook
his hand hard and thought to myself that he was much more
real than those American directors, who all seemed made from
the same mold, like the cakes from the bakery downstairs. He
said, I am about to begin shooting a new film and you would
give me great happiness if you would consent to play the leading
role, you are very beautiful and exactly suited to the part, the
girl I have imagined. I wasn't surprised; I always knew this would
happen someday. All I felt was satisfaction, as when you return
home after a long time or when you see someone you love very
much. We set a meeting for the next morning so he could tell
me about his film and we could work out all the details. When
he finished his tea, he paid and left, tall but a little stooped in
his white shirt, his star-shoes squeaking on the marble tiles, and
I cleared the table, humming some tune from the radio and saying
to myself that maybe this was the last time. I was in such a good
mood I didn't even feel like throwing a tray in the middle of the
lobby. I went into the kitchen and saw Meir leaning on the
refrigerator, his lips circled like a fish mouth blowing smoke rings
at Fawzi, whose smile was yellow with fear. Arab dog, put your
hand here, said Meir and winked at me. Fawzi thrust out his
palm, which looked like wrinkled cardboard because it was in
water so much, and Meir tapped lightly with his finger and
dropped a cigarette ash in it. I couldn't restrain myself anymore.
I grabbed a pot on the coffee machine and brought it down on
his stupid head.

3

The next day the sky was shining as if polished by a window-washer on a very tall ladder. I put on jeans and a pink shirt and went to meet my director on Dizengoff Street at the corner of Jabotinsky, as we planned. At ten on the dot a long sparkling blue Mercedes stopped next to me, and my director, his hair combed back, in a white suit, opened the door for me and said with a smile, Good morning, Malka, get in. I wanted to ask him a lot of questions such as where we were going and what the movie was about and what part I would have and what movies he had made so far, but I didn't know whether to call him Mr. Spielman or Joshua so I said nothing, instead I quietly inhaled the smell of leather upholstery mixed with the smells of aftershave and shoe polish. We parked next to a small beauty parlor I didn't know. Inside, he told me to sit in the revolving chair, stood behind me and whispered for a long time with the blond hair-dresser. I could see them in the mirror, but I closed my eyes so I could feel his fingers ruffling my hair, moving it from side to side, to show her exactly how the hairdo was supposed to be. I understood it was for the movie and I didn't interfere. They could have made me bald, I wouldn't have minded, but they only gave me a short haircut, like a boy's. I didn't recognize myself when I looked in the mirror. So that's how the girl in his imagination looks, I thought. Who is this girl in his imagination. Maybe a long-ago love.

We went to the southern part of town and stopped on one of the old streets, opposite a small theater. The wall next to the box office was covered with peeling posters for Yiddish shows. We went in the back door and down a long corridor with neon lights. Faded black-and-white pictures of actors in costumes and heavy make-up were hanging on the walls where big water spots had the shape of strange moldy-smelling animals. My director walked in front of me with big strides of his polished shoes and opened the door at the end of the corridor. We went into a big dim room. The air was very dusty and I started sneezing. *Wer ist dort?* screeched a woman's voice from the depths of the room. *Dos bin ikh*, answered my director. *Ah, Spielman, ikh kum shoyn*, said the woman. I didn't understand a word. Spellbound, I walked around the room, which looked as if they held the dance of the dead there. Long gowns of shiny cloth were hanging along the walls, next to suits, long black jackets, and Styrofoam heads with wigs and top hats and big crinkly hats trimmed with plastic flowers stared with blind eyes on the shelf above them, and heaps of shoes were lying around on the floor: high-heeled sparkly shoes, black pointy shoes, gold sandals with pieces of glass, feathery pink slippers, thick-soled soldier boots, nurse's shoes with laces, velvet slippers with silver buckles for princes, children's red shoes, and more and more empty shoes, as if their owners had just stepped out of them a minute ago and were now jumping barefoot on some lawn. The old woman, suddenly appearing between the draperies of dresses, reminded me of my grandma, with her triple chin. A huge black mole sprouted on Grandma's middle chin, and another mole, smaller, pink, was hidden in a fold between her nose and cheek, and when she was silent or sleeping you almost couldn't see it. With Spielman's old woman, the mole next to her nose was like a brake for her glasses, and her chins were wrapped with a yellow cloth measuring tape that fell on her tremendous breasts. *Vos makht dayn mame?* she croaked. *Borukh hashem, borukh hashem*, he said, then pointed at me and explained something to her in a fast whisper. All her chins wobbled with understanding, and she came up to me and started winding the yellow tape around my arms and stomach and chest, muttering to herself, *Tsvey un tsvantsik, akht un zekh-*

tsik, fineff un nayntsik. She wrote the numbers with a pencil in a small notebook, then disappeared among the dresses, and only the dim hum of a sewing machine showed she was there. My director, his hands clasped behind his back, strolled along the walls and examined the dresses as if he were at an exhibition. He stopped at a white cotton dress, took it off the hanger, put it in my hands, and said, In the meantime get into this, Malka, I'll wait for you outside. He went out and I put on the dress, which fit me perfectly. I also found a pair of white high-heeled shoes and started dancing, the white cloth skirt flapping around me like flags on Independence Day. Then I looked for a mirror to see his long-ago love in the white dress. I opened the door where the old woman had disappeared, and found myself on a stage, on the set of a ballroom in a palace—there was a winding wooden staircase covered with a faded scarlet plush carpet, and two plaster columns on either side covered with imitation marble wallpaper. At the bottom of each pillar was a big flowerpot with green plastic plants. The floor of the stage was marked with charcoal and chalk, squares of black, squares of white, and dusty purple drapes with gold tassels hung from the ceiling. At the back of the stage sat the old woman, her heavy foot moving the pedal of the sewing machine. A small table lamp poured light on her chins, which gleamed with sweat. Her black mole seemed to wink at me. I saw no mirror. I got out of there.

Spielman was waiting for me outside, leaning on the car door. From the car radio you could hear a concert. His face lit up when he saw me, and he looked young standing like that in the sun in his white suit with the top button open. You must be hungry, let's go eat, he said, opening the door for me. On the way, he glanced at me from time to time, humming along with the music. What movies have you made so far, I asked, but he didn't answer, maybe he didn't hear, he just went on humming and looking at me with his sad eyes, then suddenly he said, I want to get to know you better, and he asked me to tell him about my childhood. I told him about my grandma, who weighed two hundred and twenty pounds and how every Saturday we took her to the beach in Dad's old blue De Soto, but once, on the way back, the car couldn't carry us all so we had to get out and push, and Grandma, who had fallen asleep in the back seat, sighed, It's so hot, and fanned herself with the weekend supplement, and muttered, How come we're going so slow. He laughed and told me about his mother, who had been a famous actress in the Warsaw Yiddish theater before the War, and afterward in Israel, until one day she forgot her lines in the middle of the show and they fired her. Then she started walking around the streets with an old baby buggy collecting empty bottles and newspapers and old clothes and torn shoes, and the whole house was filled with junk, even the sink and bed and bathtub; there wasn't even room 'or her, but she wouldn't let them take anything out, she said everything was important and necessary because you never knew what might happen. Finally they locked up the house with all the trash, promised her that nothing would be removed, and put her in an old people's home. She felt good there. She performed Yiddish songs on Friday night, and had friends and admirers, and the only thing she collected were newspaper announcements about senior citizens getting married. I promised her a part in my film, he said. In movies every scene is filmed separately so you don't have to remember too many words. We drove along the Esplanade, which was almost empty at that warm hour of a weekday afternoon. Only the man selling cotton candy was sweating there in his visor cap over the tank that smelled of burnt sugar, and he waved pink clouds on sticks over his head and shouted, Cotton candy, cotton candy, while two children, maybe ten years old, were standing on white plastic chairs with their pants down having a pissing contest. When we passed the square of the old opera house, which they're renovating, Spielman said, The old Yaron movie theater was here, I saw the first films in my life here, with a little girl who agreed to be my girlfriend because I knew how to sneak into the matinees so the Yemenite usher wouldn't catch us and tell the principal. I took her to see Gary Cooper and Clark Gable and John Wayne. She loved them, gobbled up their black-and-white faces with her enormous green eyes while she sucked red soda pop through a straw. I couldn't concentrate on the film because I was waiting for the scary parts when she'd grab my arm with her little fingernails, and for the sad parts when I could take out my white handkerchief, ironed especially for the occasion, and wipe her tears. At the end of the last year of school she married a high-ranking army officer. On her wedding night I went to the movies; for the first time in my life I went alone, and for the first time I stood in line at the box office and bought a ticket. They were showing Variety Lights by an Italian director whose name I had never heard before, a soft and magical name, like a pearl necklace: Federico Fellini. Only later did I learn that that was his first film. It's about a young beauty queen who falls in love with an aging actor and decides to join his troupe traveling among wretched provincial theaters. Gradually the pictures won my heart, and I laughed in amazement because I knew those actors, in my childhood I had traveled with them to Haifa and Jerusalem and Petakh Tikvah and Hadera, to perform in small dusty auditoriums for an audience of thirty people or sometimes even five. I used to stand in the wings and watch my mother, who was a virgin named Leah or a respected and evil rich lady named Sara-Pearl or the dairyman's wife Golda, and I would smile impatiently at the applause because I knew that she'd come back to me, kiss me on my forehead, and once again become only my mother. I decided I would be a film director like Fellini and capture in the projector all the memories of my childhood, and the traitress too I would capture forever, and for a moment it seemed to me that she was smiling at me in black-and-white from the screen, and I knew that from now on she was inside me, and I stopped thinking of her at the wedding with her John Wayne.

My director looked at me and said quietly, as if to himself, You are so much like her. At Jaffa we went to a restaurant with stone walls and a high ceiling, sat next to the big arched window and looked out at a flock of gulls and the sea below. The tablecloth was purple, and pink linen napkins shaped like fans were stuck in the wineglasses that caught the sun. Everything is just right, I said to myself, and ordered three courses and coffee with whipped-cream-cake for dessert. I knew it didn't matter to him because he had to be rich, with his Mercedes. The hotel owner has a Mercedes too, but a black one. We drank wine. The waitress showed him the bottle with the label, then poured a little in his glass to taste, and after he said, Excellent, she poured for both of us. She doesn't know I'm a waitress too, I laughed to myself, but then remembered that I was a movie star now, so I sipped the wine slowly, held the glass with three fingers and lifted my pinkie. Are you familiar with Fellini's films, he asked. I said I hadn't seen Fellini's films, only movies in English, An Officer and a Gentleman, Saturday Night Fever, things like that. Over the years he has become one of the most important directors in the world, he said. For almost twenty years I saw all his films, collected every scrap of information about him, everything in the papers, and waited for a chance to meet him, to prove with my own eyes that it could be. And then one day in 1969 I read in the paper that Fellini would be the guest of honor at the film festival in Venice. My director's face beamed from

the light of the movie projector of his memory when he told me
how he went there especially to meet him, even if only for a
minute, because he had to ask him one question: Signor Fellini,
are you happy. He waited for him all day in the lobby of the
magnificent Grand Hotel—crystal chandeliers, purple velvet
armchairs, Carrara marble tables—and recited this question to
himself in Italian, and after eleven cups of espresso he suddenly
saw him coming down the staircase in a tuxedo and shiny black
shoes, holding onto the arm of his wife the actress Giulietta
Masina, who wore a long evening gown with a sky-blue train
that flowed from the top of the staircase to the bottom. Fellini
stood still a moment and smiled at the cameras that flickered
and flashed in his leonine face; he ran his hand through his
graying mane and told the journalists hunched piously over their
little notebooks about his new film Satyricon, which was about
to open the festival. Then Spielman went to him at the foot of
the stairs, and Fellini smiled generously and inclined his big ear
to listen, but from so much excitement Spielman forgot the
question he had been reciting to himself all day in Italian, and
just stood there repeating like a parrot, Signor Fellini, Signor
Fellini, Signor Fellini, and Fellini apparently understood because
he said *Sì, sì*, grabbed his arm and pulled him to go with them,
with him and Giulietta. Spielman's breath stopped at the sight
of the blue Mercedes waiting at the door of the hotel, as long
and sleek as a whale, and the chauffeur, in a white uniform with
gold stripes on the cuffs, a visor cap, and white gloves, opened
the door for them with a deep bow, and Spielman vowed that
he too would have a Mercedes like that someday. The conversation then flowed freely, in English, and he told Fellini that he
was a film director from Israel, and he even gave him a small
piece of technical advice, and Fellini was very happy and promised to use it in his next film, and as a sign of gratitude Fellini

invited him to the premiere of Satyricon. Spielman was embarrassed and said he wasn't dressed properly for the opening night of an international film festival. Fellini asked his chauffeur to turn on the light, and he and Giulietta examined him and said that his black suit was all right even if it was a little faded, and his shirt was at least clean. Giulietta said in her melodious accent that his striped tie was dreadful, it made him look like an accountant, but it would do for the evening. The only problem was his brown shoes, because it wouldn't do to be seen at such an event in shoes that weren't black; everyone in the audience would consider brown shoes a personal affront, a violation of all the rules, bad form. It was like a widow going to her husband's funeral in a red dress, said Giulietta. Spielman told them that he didn't have any other shoes, not even in the pensione where he was staying, and he said sadly, Thank you for the invitation, I'll see the film some other time. Then Fellini bent over heavily, took off his black shoes, straightened up, his face flushed from the effort, and said, Try these on. Spielman took off his embarrassing brown shoes, trying to hide the little hole in his sock, and put on Fellini's black ones, which fit perfectly, and he was filled with an enormous joy. Fellini put on Spielman's brown shoes and said, They can't keep me out of the premiere of my own film, and he laughed and recalled the War when all the young men in his town had to join the Fascist youth movement, but he protested by always coming in brown shoes instead of the black ones that were part of the uniform. Then Fellini opened the little bar next to the seat and poured whiskey for the three of them, and they clinked glasses, and by the time they arrived at the Lido auditorium they weren't Signor Fellini and Signor Spielman anymore but Federico and Joshua, amici.

He went on and told how the audience cheered and parted to make way for them when they entered the most magnificent movie palace he was ever in, and a brass band with an accordion burst into Nino Rota's melodies from Fellini's film, which gripped your heart with melancholy gaiety, and he wandered there dazzled by the beauty of the women and the splendor of the men, and the sparkling jewels and champagne glasses, and was drunk on the smell of cigarettes and fine perfume, and in spite of his threadbare suit and accountant's tie he felt taller than everyone, as if the shoes had overcome the force of gravity, and he couldn't concentrate on the film because he felt the soles of his feet burning. When the screening was over, when his new friend appeared on the stage and bowed deeply and everyone applauded as if they didn't notice the brown shoes on his feet, Spielman applauded more than anyone, until his hands were burning and tears came into his eyes. Afterward, he was pushed outside with the audience streaming toward the Grand Canal, and he stood in the first row waiting with everyone for the triumphal cruise of the great director and his wife, and when the gondola bedecked with necklaces of colored lights passed by him and Fellini and Giulietta were sitting in it and waving to the cheering Venetians who flung roses at them, Spielman took off the shoes and waved them to catch Fellini's attention, and the firm warm voice rising out of the darkness and soaring over the bravos of the crowd said, Keep them for now; someday, when I visit your country, I'll come get them. The glittering gondola departed, disappeared down the canal, Giulietta's sky-blue train waving in the wind, and Spielman whispered, Ciao, Federico, and he put the fine leather Italian shoes back on, and when he finished tying the laces and straightened up, the canal was black empty water and the shouts of the crowd had also died away, and then he remembered that he hadn't asked all evening, Signor Fellini, are you happy. That was the encounter that changed my life, he said, and the projector of his memory went off.

A big gull flew into the restaurant through the window and soared to the ceiling with a frantic beating of wings. The customers and waiters stared in surprise and with panicky smiles. The gull hesitated a moment then landed on our table and scrutinized us sharply. Spielman gave it a piece of bread, and the gull snatched it up in its yellow beak and took off outside. We watched it until it disappeared over the sea. And Federico, I asked with my mouth full of marvelous whipped-cream-cake. Federico hasn't come yet, said Spielman. I walk in his shoes all the time, these are my lucky shoes. I polish them every day, and once a year I give them to a shoemaker, something needs fixing, a sole needs to be replaced. I know that one day a blue Mercedes will stop in front of my house, long and sleek as a whale, and all the neighbors will peer down from their balconies and be amazed at the sight of the chauffeur in a white uniform opening the car door with a deep bow. And he'll get out with his heavy body, a little older than I remember him, his mane whiter, and he'll smile his famous leonine smile and cross the yard with long strides and ring the doorbell of my apartment, and I'll open the door and I won't be in the least surprised, because this is the moment I've been waiting for, and I'll say, Federico, and he'll say, Joshua, amico. Then I'll give him back the shoes and he'll whistle with admiration and say, How well you took care of them all these years. Just like new. My director fell silent, and suddenly he looked old and sad. I knew there was no point in asking any more questions. We finished our coffee and he paid. I wanted to take something from there, a wineglass or a silver spoon. Whenever I'm in a nice place where I'm happy, I always want to take something as a souvenir. But I didn't. People don't understand, they call it stealing and make a big fuss. We drove silently along the beach. The cotton candy man wasn't on the Esplanade now, but a few pink sugar clouds remained in the sky.

Spielman stopped at my house and before I got out he looked at me for a long time, as if he saw something there which no one before him had ever seen. Cautiously he stroked my short hair in its new cut, then said, You know, Malka, in the soul there are no wrinkles.

4

We sat on yellow plastic chairs at the end of a long corridor on the second floor of City Hall facing a brown door. In the middle of a formica plate were the black letters S. Kornfield. We were waiting to see Mr. Kornfield of the Education Department. Spielman hoped to get financial support for his film from Korn-field and had wanted me to come along. Your beauty will melt any man's heart, even the heart of a city official, he said with his warm smile. I asked him to tell me, while we waited, some-thing about the film, but he grew mysterious and said that Fellini never revealed the subject of his films to his actors before shoot-ing; every night he'd give them a page with their lines for the next day, and that's how he got spontaneity in acting. So I sat there swinging my feet and reading the name S. Kornfield for the hundredth time and trying to make words out of the letters of the name. At first I only got annoying words—drone, fork, fink—and I told myself we wouldn't be getting any money out of this Kornfield, but then I found a few good words—life, dine, finer—and I became more optimistic. I told Spielman that in my opinion it was outrageous to make an important director like him wait such a long time and not even offer him a cup of coffee. He stood up, knocked on the door, opened it a crack, and stuck his head inside. I could hear the secretary tell him in her chewing-gum voice that yes, they had made an appointment for nine-thirty and it was now after ten-thirty, but something urgent came up and Kornfield is terribly busy now and she really doesn't know when he'll be available, so either you wait or leave, sir, but do close the door because of the air conditioning. Spielman closed the door, came back, and sat next to me with a sad smile. His long thin hair slipped to the side like a withered plant and exposed his baldness. You're bored, he said quietly, so I'll tell you about next year's Venice Festival, when this film of ours will represent Israel and win the Golden Palm. He pulled me to the other end of the corridor, to the window, pointed down at the big fountain in the square in front of City Hall and said in the voice of a television announcer: We are over the Grand Canal, and yes, there are the great director Spielman and Malka his star getting out of the gondola now and entering Lido Palace to the cheers of the crowd. Then he put his arm through mine, walked proudly down the corridor, and continued: As you can see, they are proceeding up the red carpet and smiling at the throng as the Venice Firemen's Orchestra plays a rousing march. He whistled a march to himself, bowed in all directions, and sat me ceremoniously on a yellow plastic chair as if it were a deep velvet armchair, and sat down next to me, smiling modestly to an invisible admirer on the other side. Then he pointed to the dirty-white wall of the corridor and went on: And now the screen is lit and the film that has won the Golden Palm, Joshua Spielman's film, begins with a Hasidic melody. He closed his eyes and started humming, *Ay bi bi bibam bi bi bibam*. The door opened and the secretary, accompanied by a gust of cold air, shouted, Stop that. Spielman opened his eyes and all the light left his face. She turned her mighty tight-skirted rear end to us and disappeared down the stairs, leaving behind her the clacking of heels and the smell of perfume, then only the smell of perfume, until it evaporated in our noses, but after a long silence we smelled it again, and heard the clacking, and she appeared carrying in front of her big bosom a tray with a fish, half a lemon,

white rice and baby carrots on a blue plastic plate, and a can of
Coke. She glanced at us as if to say, You're still here, and shut
the door that said S. Kornfield. At about one-thirty, after we
had given up hope, the door opened again and the secretary
minced, You can go in now. We went in. We sat down. Kornfield, behind the desk, looked exactly like his name: silvery hair
combed back, glasses, a sharp nose, thin lips, a narrow tie, and
a gold tiepin with a pearl. The window behind him was like a
painting, blue sky with a small gray cloud. The plastic plate lay
on a corner of the desk, and from it the fish skeleton peered
sorrowfully out of one eye. Kornfield diligently cleaned his teeth
with a toothpick, then broke the toothpick in two, again in two,
put the pieces in the ashtray, took a new toothpick from the
drawer, and as he dug between his teeth he said, I read your
screenplay, Mr. Spielman, yes. Very interesting, yes, but I don't
see anything that would draw an audience, no. The Yiddish
theater is an old subject, a dead subject, not for the living, no,
why wake the dead when there are so many contemporary subjects for films, such as social injustice in the city or the drug
problem among our youth or the collapse of the health care
system. If you really want to do a film on the subject of culture
and art, we do have a wonderful orchestra, you know, fine mu-
seums, even opera, yes, why don't you do a film about our opera.
Our purpose, you see, is to support films that deal with subjects
of public interest, yes, but your subject is personal, peripheral,
so my answer is no. He broke the toothpick in two, again in
two, put the pieces in the ashtray, and took a new toothpick
from the drawer. In the window behind him there was now only
blue sky, the gray cloud had come inside and settled on Spielman's face. We stood up. Spielman said, Goodbye and thank
you very much. Leaving, we heard S. Kornfield's voice, Good
luck to you. It was very hot outside, and the fountain in the

square in front of City Hall was only a fountain, not a canal, not Venice.

We got into the car, drove off, and I thought to myself, The Mercedes must be worth a lot, why doesn't he sell it and use the money for the film, but you shouldn't poke your nose into other people's business. We stopped on Allenby Street, not far from the sea, by a movie house I didn't know. Behind glass there were photographs of a naked blond woman with enormous breasts and tiny gold stars instead of nipples. In one photograph there was a bigger star between her spread thighs with Flaming Mimi written on it in black. Mimi's hair was wet, scraggly, her eyes were half closed, and her red tongue stuck out over her upper lip as if she was trying to touch the tip of her nose with it. In another photograph Mimi was on all fours wearing nothing but long red stockings, and a giant naked black man crouched behind her holding her white breasts with his black hands, his face twisted in an effort to push into her a very big gold star that had Ecstasy of Lust written on it. Her tongue here was stretched to the side as if she were trying to lick her own ear. I stopped for a moment to look, but Spielman pulled my hand impatiently and said, Come on. Either the photographs didn't interest him or else he had already seen them many times. We went into a gloomy stairwell and I had to hold my nose because of the sharp smell of urine, and I didn't let go of it until we reached the cellar and a door with Shein Productions on it. Spielman opened the door and we went in. A dark girl who sat at a desk typing glanced at us with raised eyebrows, smiled thinly to herself, and said, Oh, Mr. Fellini, how are you, what's new in cinecitta. The walls were covered with posters of old Israeli movies. I had seen one of them when I was little, a movie with Uri Zohar before he grew a beard and sidelocks and turned into a rabbi in Jerusalem. Albert here, asked Spielman fearfully. Now where can he be,

dark girl indifferently, addressing the white sheet in the type-
writer. We went through a door with the sign A. Shein, Producer, and into a room whose scarred walls had no posters and
not even a window. Big feet in shabby brown shoes were on the
desk among three black telephones; behind the shoes we could
see the sweaty face of Albert the Producer, who was sound asleep.
His thick eyebrows were pinched with two plastic clothespins,
a red one and a blue one, which sprouted from his head like
horns, and his thinning hair was scattered in the wind from a
rusty fan that wearily turned left and right. I started laughing.
Albert opened a pair of frightened blue eyes, immediately smiled
like a baby and said, Oh it's you. He stood up ponderously, big
wet rings on his shirt, and I couldn't figure out what color it was.
He shook my hand and said, The young lady laughs because of
the clothespins, but I need them to concentrate. And when I
leave the office, I use them to clip my pants so the cuffs don't
get caught in the chain of my bike. Ask him, and he pointed
his chin at Spielman, who nodded politely and said, What's new.
Good news, good news, Albert chanted, there's an investor for
your film. Yes, who, asked Spielman without much faith. A bank,
said Albert portentously. A bank? Spielman was dumbfounded.
The manager of a bank is willing to put a hundred thousand into
your film, Albert said solemnly and licked the sweat off his upper
lip. Spielman took a deep breath and his eyes began to gleam.
But, Albert pointed a plump pinkie choked in a gold ring, there's
a condition. What condition, asked Spielman, suspicious. In the
last scene, Albert said, where the old director of the troupe, your
mother, finally marries her nebbikhl, and they fly off over the
buildings in a balloon like a Chagall painting, and she sings her
song about the birds, the bank manager wants the name and
logo of the bank on the balloon, in gold. That shall never come
to pass, cried Spielman in Biblical anger. The wedding of my

mother and Fayvl under the huppah of a bank? You destroy my film, he shouted, gesturing in despair. Nobody's destroying anything, Albert also shouted, and the blood rushed to his face. He paced the room, an enraged bull with one red horn and one blue one. Forty years I've known you, forty years you've wanted to make your film. Twenty years you waited to meet that Italian, whose name I don't want to mention, and another twenty you looked for a maydele for your leading actress. You don't have another twenty years to come up with the money. Worms will be eating your kishkes before you make your film. He unclipped the red clothespin and waved it menacingly in Spielman's face as if he were going to clamp his nose. And who'll want to invest in such a film, tell me, who. No sex in it, no action, no politics, just balloons and old people who talk Yiddish. I tell you, this is your last chance. Take the money from the bank. I won't, yelled Spielman. Take it, Albert coaxed. No, said Spielman, stubborn, and to me he said, Let's go. We went out to the street. Spielman trembled as if it were terribly cold. There will be a film, Malka, I promise you, there will be a film, he whispered through teeth that chattered. There will be a film, I said. I pulled him into a strip of sunshine on the sidewalk and hugged him. He stopped trembling. There will be a film, I said again. I knew what I had to do.

5

I got to work on time that day, even though I left home late and waited at the corner of Dizengoff and Jabotinsky for two lights to change, in case an old woman showed up with a pirate's red kerchief around her neck and asked me to help her cross the street. But no parrot-faced old woman came to take me for a walk and sing to me in Yiddish, so I went to the hotel, my stomach jumping because of what was waiting for me there. The last I saw Meir, he was passed out on the kitchen floor among broken pieces of coffeepot, his forehead dripping blood that looked like ketchup. It was only two days ago but it seemed like a thousand years. I hoped he wasn't dead.

The guard at the employees' entrance sat in his little booth, eating a tuna sandwich and watching the basketball game on television. As the timeclock punched my card 4:45, I thought, Maybe he will be a hotel doorkeeper, because if you want something enough it does come true in the end. In the dressing room I decided not to put makeup on my eyes. Let them be big, so what. I went up to the lobby, my heart pounding fast, and on the way ran into Fedida, who bared his Bugs Bunny teeth in a smile as if nothing had happened. In the distance I saw Rita leaning at the bar, shifting her weight from leg to leg, blinking, sucking something, and Meir looking at her anxiously over the beer tap, a big bump on his forehead. A heavy stone fell from my heart and a small pebble of disappointment took its place. I walked around, so he wouldn't see me, and went into the kitchen. Fawzi's head wasn't at the slot window for the dishes. There was another head instead, wreathed with black curls. I'm Mahmoud, said the head and smiled a white smile at me. I'm Millie, I said, where's Fawzi? Gone, said Mahmoud and lifted his eyes to the ceiling. What do you mean gone, where did he go? Mahmoud spread his arms, I don't know, I'm here now. I went to Meir, who looked at me with a leer. Where's Fawzi, I asked. Fired, said Meir smiling, and lit a cigarette. Why, I asked. He hit me with a coffeepot, he said and dragged on his cigarette with pleasure. But I did that, I whispered. I felt that I was falling from a high cliff. I know, said Meir quietly, and blew a smoke ring at me. Besides, he dirtied the ceiling, he added. Dirtied the ceiling, I asked. Go see for yourself, he said. I opened the door to the storeroom, which was more a closet than a room, and looked up. The ceiling was covered with pictures of birds, spread wings: parrots and gulls, sparrows and doves, storks and cranes, finches and pink flamingos, and there were big bold birds I had never seen in my life, including one blue-and-white peacock that had a woman's breasts. You could almost hear the beating of wings, the chirping, the mating calls. I could see Fawzi at night; instead of sleeping, he would lie on his back on the dishwasher and draw, slowly and lovingly, a bird a night. Pretty, said Mahmoud, his eyes raised and sparkling. But Meir's head thrust through the slot. Tomorrow they're painting the ceiling, he said with satisfaction, and to Mahmoud he said, Arab Dog put out your hand. Mahmoud's eyes died at once. He put out his hand, which looked like wrinkled cardboard from all the water, and Meir tapped his cigarette ash into it.

At table 48 sat the five giants and seven dwarfs, plus Snow White and the prince and the silver-haired director. But I didn't even look at them. I had a more important mission. A mission everything depended on. Meanwhile, I went to Mrs. Brown at table 27. She lifted her brown eyes from the menu and asked, What do you have today? I recited the whole menu to her, in order, and went to bring her a pot of boiling water for her camomile tea. On the way I passed table 29 and saw that Mr. Gordon and his black nurse weren't sitting there looking at each other with melting eyes over their five-o'clock tea. Mr. Gordon passed away yesterday, Fedida told me. Tears filled my eyes. They say he left everything to the nurse, Fedida went on, and not a thing to his children, who are threatening to sue. And they're perfectly right. To throw your money away on some black woman and not leave a cent to your own flesh and blood. He was a little cuckoo at the end. And Fedida twirled a finger at his temple. Just as I served Mrs. Brown her pot of boiling water and her cup, I was called to the phone. Could you please bring, said the hotel owner, a smoked salmon sandwich, a glass of orange juice, and a pot of coffee up to my office. Of course, of course. Excited, I cut the sandwich into the most precise quarters in the world and squeezed the oranges myself. In the elevator to the top floor, I shut my eyes, crossed my fingers, and prayed. The hotel owner observed me quietly above his desk and Znaforts, beneath the desk, fixed his blind eyes on me as I rolled the wagon in and put the dishes on the glass table with trembling hands. I tried not to spill anything, but a little orange juice dripped on my hand, which I wiped on the back of my dress and hoped he hadn't noticed. The hotel owner opened his wallet with his one hand, to give me my tip, but I went up to him as I had prepared, and said, Wait, can I ask you something. I'm listening, he said, and Znaforts's ears perked up. I told him everything, as if he were my father. I told him about Spielman and the film Spielman was trying to make about his mother and the Yiddish theater. I described the wedding in the balloon, like the Chagall on the wall behind him. I told him about the meeting with Fellini and even about the shoes. I told about S. Kornfield at City Hall and Albert the Producer. I talked a-mile-a-minute, knowing this was our last chance. The hotel owner watched me with a strange look, then said, How much do you need. A hundred thousand dollars, I whispered. Znaforts scratched his head with his front paw, but the hotel owner took out a leather-covered checkbook and wrote a check. For a moment I couldn't breathe. I couldn't believe this was happening. I reached for the check, but he said, Wait, and put it under his gold paperweight. I need you to help me take off my jacket. He's hot, I said to myself. Even he doesn't write such a big check every day. I helped him take off his jacket, very careful with the pink arm, as if it hurt, and laid the jacket nicely on the carved chair back. Now help me with my tie, he said. Znaforts bared his gums in a doggy smile. I thought he could do that himself, but didn't say anything. I undid the tie, which was the same pink as the arm, and set it carefully on the jacket. Now the shirt, he said, closing his eyes. I opened the diamond stickpin and unbuttoned the white shirt. He wants to sleep with me, I suddenly thought. A sweet smell rose from his smooth cheeks. He got out of his shirtsleeves, impatient now, and put the shirt too on the chair back. Znaforts huffed, his red tongue hanging long, like a demon's. Then the hotel owner took off the rubber band of the artificial arm and dropped the arm to the rug, pink palm to the ceiling. With his eyes closed, he showed his thin stump, which was twisted and scarred, and whispered, Touch it. I froze. The statues of goat idols whirled around me, their eyes winking in mockery. Touch it just once, pleaded the barechested hotel owner, his eyes shut and his face tormented. I turned and ran and didn't wait for the elevator but went down all seventeen flights of stairs, my heart hammering wildly.

I leaned against the wall, gasping. As in a horror film, the people sitting at the tables grew transparent, as if I had X-ray eyes. Under the expensive clothes, with the labels of the best fashion designers of Europe, I could see folds of fat, pimples. The sandwiches and petits fours that disappeared into politely closed and lipsticked mouths were ground by rotting teeth, slid down the digestive tract, and in the stomach mixed with stuff the color of vomit. I saw the bald skull under the silver toupee of the Hollywood director, and inside his skull Snow White lay naked and spread-eagled, tied to a bed and with her mouth taped. And in Snow White's skull too she was spread-eagled, and the black basketball player's behind was rising and falling like a chocolate muffin between her legs. But in the black basketball player's skull he was holding a loving cup carried high by his teammates. Inside the skull of a fat man eating a cheese sandwich I saw the enormous ice cream he would order for dessert, and in his wife's skull she was wearing a blue gown covered with the diamonds of the woman at the next table. In Mrs. Brown's skull were German words, *nein, Schwein, danke schön*. In the skull of the pale piano player I saw a malignant tumor and three hundred-shekel bills. In the skull of the old European was his wife, with whom he waltzed every evening on the small dance floor, but she was on the kitchen floor with a bread knife in her heart; and in her skull, resting on his shoulder, was a childhood memory. She is a little girl lying on a riverbank in a green grove and a little blond boy pops cherries into her mouth. In Rita's skull, Rita was in a white wedding gown carried in the arms of Meir in a black suit, a photographer leaping around them in the garden of the hotel, recording their bliss against the sunset.

I looked out the window and saw the sea swell and overflow the shore. A salt wind whistled in awful nasal rage, and wet-rag dirty clouds choked the light, and the green water rose higher, and waves high as mountains invaded the patio of the swimming pool and the tennis courts, sweeping rackets and green balls and chaise longues and parasols and bottles of suntan lotion and Scandinavian tourists with their paperback Agatha Christie murder mysteries and sunglasses and towels and beach clogs and Walkman sets, and an inner tube with a duck's head and a little boy in it, and the lifeguard and his whistle. Now with their white tongues the waves are devouring the windowpanes and bursting in and flooding the chairs of the lobby and the rugs and the chandeliers, and the pots fill with water and sink with a plop, and decorated plates and cups float and collide with the ping of china, and spongecakes sponge up water and also sink, and knives and forks and spoons sink too, and packets of instant coffee and sugar and saccharine and mint-flavored or cinnamon-flavored toothpicks and furs and whimpering society ladies and purses

containing lipsticks and tampons and checkbooks and credit
cards and headache pills and invitations to fashion shows and
keys to houses and cars, and businessmen sink, their gold pens
and appointment books and pipes, and a wave pulls the silver
wig off the director's head and sticks it on Rita's chin like a curly
beard. He covers his baldness with his hands, then swallows
water and chokes, and the star closes her eyes and hopes it won't
ruin her makeup, now that she has a chance to play Ophelia.
She fills with water, expanding like a rubber doll, while the
dwarfs climb onto the shoulders of the giants, but the water rises
and covers the giants too, and ashtrays and menus spin in the
whirlpool with Members of the Knesset and bottles of wine and
whiskey and gin, and a red high-heeled shoe and maraschino
cherries and bartenders and ice cubes and pairs of dancers doing
a slow waltz as they drown. The white grand piano bobs in the
water and sinks slowly with the piano player and his tumor, and
the green water overwhelms the reception clerks coughing in
three languages and the cashiers and the colorful money and the
elevator boys, their red peaked hats floating for a moment on
the surface. The groom and the photographer and the rabbi do
a dog paddle, the bride's veil on the rabbi's face, his black sidelocks showing under the veil, and the water rolls and rages and
enters the kitchens and swallows up bunches of grapes and wa-
termelons and feta cheese and frying pans and frozen fish and
chickens and mice and worms and lemons and cans and can
openers and omelets and dishwashers and artichokes and pickles
and strict supervisors of Kashrut and jars of Beluga caviar and
poppyseed cookies. Rising higher and higher, it floods each floor
and penetrates each room and drowns pink nightgowns and beds
and diamond earrings and suitcases and keys to suitcases and
hangers and blankets and pillows and sheets and hair dryers and
cameras and Japanese tourists and nailfiles and vitamin capsules

and telephones and combs and soaps and bras and moisturizing cream and candy and vaseline and used condoms and colored contact lenses and sleeping pills and televisions and teddy bears and stuffed giraffes and children sinking into their last dream, not understanding why they're wet. And a stethoscope floats away, and a doctor, and deodorants and sprays for bad breath and watches and evening gowns and hair rollers and pictures by artists of Safed and Jerusalem and showercaps and pornographic magazines and chess sets and nylon stockings with runs in them and a skateboard and a set of false teeth and bandaids and matches and fire extinguishers and men and women clinging to each another and Q-tips and a king and jack and ace and joker and a seven of clubs and hearing aids and bathrobes and peacock feathers and jockstraps and bubble bath that makes colored foam and chambermaids and stationery and monkey wrenches and typewriters and exercycles and an Indian masseur and a pack of cigarettes. The hotel owner tries to stay above the water clutching his pink plastic arm, Save me save me, while Znaforts goes under with a doggy smile and a check for a hundred thousand dollars in his teeth, and the assistant hotel manager and his secretary are also drawn into the whirlpool, with Coke bottles and janitors and telephone operators and house slippers and toothbrushes. The entire hotel now is sinking, all seventeen stories, all six hundred thirty-two rooms, and the parking lot and the cars and the chauffeurs and the doormen and the guard at the employees' entrance, and the wind spins thirteen white chef's hats and feeds them to the waves, which stir them into a paper gruel, but Fawzi's birds take off from the ceiling, they alone, the parrots and gulls, sparrows and doves, storks and cranes, finches and pink flamingos, beautiful bright birds, all except the peacock who can't fly, they open their wings and soar above the flood, shrieking lamentations until they disappear into the clouds. Only then does the sea calm, and doze, blue and sated, caressed by a breeze, and a tanned lifeguard peers out and hangs a white flag of all-clear on the pole of his tower.

6

We drove out to visit Mrs. Spielman, Joshua's mother, in the old age home. Outside the city there were orange groves, and the sky stretched above them with a blue yawn. Between the orange groves and the sky lay the stillness of the Sabbath eve. On the way I told Joshua about the hotel owner and how I ran without taking the check, but he said nothing, only nodded.

The old age home greeted us with the smell of mown grass and the swishing of sprinklers. We dashed between the sprays but our feet got wet anyway. Joshua anxiously examined Fellini's shoes, shook his head and said, Water's not good for them. When we got to the culture hall, we heard a piano and singing, and Joshua said, That's my mother, and his face lit up with a childish smile. We poked our heads in the door and saw her standing on a stage above a sea of silver heads. She was wearing a dress sprinkled with large flowers, red, gold, and blue, and had a red beret cocked over her forehead. Yellow wisps of hair hung from it, and her blue eyes twinkled. I could have sworn she was the one who took me for a walk on Dizengoff a few days ago and made me late to work. An old hunchback with long white hair was bent over the piano, bent so low, his ear almost touched the keys. But his beautiful white fingers skipped over them as nimbly as mice. She sang in Yiddish, a sweet soft voice full of longing:

> *Vu bistu geven ven di yugent iz geven,*
> *Un dos harts hot mit libe gebrent?*
> *Haynt bistu do ven der kop is shoyn gro*
> *Un es tsitern bay mir shoyn di hent.*

She sang again, and the whole silver sea sang with her, swaying, and then there was an explosion of applause. Then the old people all lined up in front of the stage where the singer sat in an armchair, and one by one they came up on the stage, and the old men put their lips to her outstretched hand and the old women kissed her on the cheek. This is how they pay her, Joshua whispered to me. Every Friday night she sings to them, then sits and collects their kisses. The line was long, three hundred people of the old age home, three hundred kisses. The last old man was especially daring; he took her face in his trembling hands and kissed her on the lips. She shook a finger at him but her blue beetles twinkled with joy. And here's my son too, she said and came over to us. I was confused a moment. You speak Hebrew, I whispered. I looked hard at her face, the red mouth, the parrot nose, but wasn't completely sure. After fifty years in Israel how could I not speak Hebrew, she laughed, and her eyes leaped cunningly. But you were on Dizengoff Street this week and you sang at the fountain, I whispered. Had I made the whole thing up? She shook her head. I haven't been out in a long time, she said sadly, in a very long time. It would be wonderful to go to Dizengoff and have some ice cream. Will you take me to Tel Aviv for ice cream? she asked like a spoiled girl. I'll take you, Joshua promised and looked at her tenderly, as soon as I finish the film. Her face changed, her eyes flashed sparks, and she shouted, Every week you say the film, the film, the leading role you promised me, the wedding in the balloon. I tell myself every morning, all right, we won't die today, we'll wait a little longer, even though all my friends are up there. She poked at the sky with a crooked finger. They're all up there calling me, Valentino and Majohin and Clark Gable, and the beautiful Vivien, and Bogart and Cooper and Garbo in her black hat, and that co-median with the mustache and cane whose mother was a Jew, all the great artistes of the Hollywood cinema. Without me they can't start shooting. I won't wait for you much longer. She pulled her finger out of the hole in the sky and waved it in his face. Even if you are my son and I am your mother, there's a limit to what I'm willing to do for you. And she turned her back and left the auditorium with the strut of a prima donna. We went out to the lawn, where we saw her sitting on a green bench in a garden. She held a white daisy and was pulling out petals one by one, muttering to herself, *Yo, neyn, yo, neyn, yo.* Who is that, she asked suddenly, pointing at me. That's Malka, mother, she's in our film, said Joshua affectionately and sat down next to her. She went on pulling the petals, then sang in a whisper to the orphaned stalk:

> *Her nor du shayn maydele,*
> *Her nor du fayn maydele,*
> *Vos vestu ton in aza vaytn veg?*

Big tears flowed down her cheeks. Joshua put his arm around her and whispered consolations in Yiddish which I didn't understand.

Then the air was filled with ringing. A hand holding a big bell appeared at a window of the white building in the center of the lawn. Old people in their best clothes hurried down paths, almost running, toward the hand with the bell. Dinner, announced Mrs. Spielman. She stood up, threw away the stripped daisy, smoothed her dress, adjusted her hat, and began to march energetically to the dining hall. The old man who had kissed her on the lips passed us, toddling along in khaki shorts and sandals with socks; he caught up with her, put his arm through hers. Joshua, watching them walk off, said in a deep, solemn voice, "He maketh my feet like hinds' feet, and setteth me upon my high places. Thou hast enlarged my steps under me, that my feet did not slip." His eyes shone gold, and the long wisps of his hair waved in the wind of the Sabbath eve, making him look like one of those ancient prophets.

7

Now you're there, and I'm here in your apartment, which is only a room, a dark dusty little room on the ground floor with a squeaky metal bed and sweaty sheets, and one chair, and a dirty gas burner on top of a small refrigerator in the corner. There's half a loaf of green bread and an empty can of beans, and in the middle of the room an old projector and a pile of round tin cans with writing in black felt-tip markers: Fellini Amarcord, Fellini Roma, Fellini Casanova, Fellini Nights of Cabiria, Fellini La Dolce Vita, Fellini, Fellini, Fellini. I'll probably have time to see every film a hundred times before you get back. It was pure chance that I saw the newspaper on Sunday morning. I don't usually read newspapers, but I felt like seeing again your old movie house on the Esplanade, where it all began, so I went there on bus 21 and sat facing the back, and the man opposite me was reading the paper, and there in the lower left-hand corner of the back page I saw a picture of you. You wore a black leather jacket I hadn't seen before and yellow sneakers, and your eyes were dull and strange under a checkered cap. Over the picture, in thick letters, it said: Box Office Robbery in Tel Aviv Thwarted. I bent over close and read the small print:

At midnight Friday the Tel Aviv police arrested Joshua Spielman, who in the fifties and sixties directed short films for the Jewish Agency, in an armed robbery attempt at the movie theater near Dizengoff Square. The crime was thwarted by quick-thinking veteran ticket seller Aharon Klein. Klein told our reporter: I was about to lock up the box office and go home when suddenly the assailant, a red kerchief over his mouth, stuck a gun in the window and said Hands up in English. I don't know English but I've seen a lot of movies so I put my hands up. The assailant gave me a child's lunchbox and asked in fancy talk for the day's take. I pretended to put the money in the box but actually pushed the alarm button with my foot. The guard came right away and took the gun from the assailant. While the guard went for the police, I kept an eye on the assailant, who did a lot of sweating and promised not to run away, so I let him go into the theater for a few minutes to see some of the new film The Interview by Federico Fellini until the police came. According to the police, Spielman also has a stolen Mercedes they have been trying to locate for weeks. The suspect requested that his arrest not be revealed to his mother who resides in a home for the aged. The indictment against Spielman will be served this week in district court.

I looked up from the paper and saw that the world was in black-and-white, no color, the trees, people, cars, sky, everything. I changed buses and went straight to the jail in Jaffa.

You sat there in the black leather jacket and the yellow sneakers, tears in your eyes, and scratched the white stubble on your cheeks. We were silent. There was nothing to say. You gave me the key to the apartment. I hung it on a chain around my neck, under my blouse. Don't worry, I said, I'll keep them for you as long as necessary. And you also leaned over and said in a hasty whisper, Go see my mother on Friday, tell her I have to be in Italy for a while because of the film and she should wait, tell her she should wait, we'll begin shooting as soon as I get back. I'll tell her, I said, and kissed your wisps of hair. You held my hand tight, shaking, and tears fell from your eyes like stars, a sparkling star in each black shoe in my hands. If only you had put them on that night, I thought sadly, the lucky shoes you always wore, instead of those yellow sneakers for thieves. I shine them again with a brush and a rag. The sharp smell of shoe polish tickles my nose, and I look out the window, waiting for the blue Mercedes, long and sleek as a whale, to stop in front of your building, and for a chauffeur in a white uniform to open the car door with a deep bow. Then he'll get out, your friend, and smile his leonine smile, cross the yard, and ring the bell, and I'll open the door and hand him the shoes, and he'll whistle in admiration and say, How well you took care of them all these years. Just like new. Then he'll ask about you and I'll tell him everything, and he'll be furious and say, Come on. And we'll go in the blue Mercedes to the prison and he'll shout, I'm Federico Fellini, and bang the desk with his heavy fist and scatter millions of lire here and there. Then the three of us will sit in the restaurant in Jaffa, the one with the purple tablecloths and the gulls, and I'll tell you about your mother, how I went to the old age home at dusk on Friday as I promised you. But there was no singing in the culture hall; the old people were sitting there, rows and rows of them, looking at an empty stage and listening to the silence. Where's Mrs. Spielman, I whispered to the old man in the khaki shorts who had kissed her on the lips. Left, he said, a few days ago, she put on her coat, took her purse, went out through the gate, and didn't come back. I went to Dizengoff Square. She's there, I knew, performing at the fountain. But only the birds on the wires were screeching; the old people dozed on the benches all alone. You'll hear this and your forehead will wrinkle with worry, but Federico will turn to the sea, point up, and say, Look. Then we'll look and see the balloon, and in it your mother waving to us in her white wedding gown. On her reddish head is a long veil playing in the wind, and a little Jew in a black suit and hat stands beside her, a dignified smile on his face, and the balloon rises higher, and she tosses us the bouquet and sings a song in Yiddish while her bridegroom accompanies her on the violin all the way to the Hollywood in heaven.

Meanwhile I wrap the shoes in paper and put them in a box, and put the brush and the polish back in the drawer, and close the shutters to make it dark, and sit at the projector and thread the first film in the pile of cans. White petals spin in the spring wind, and a beautiful Italian woman, all in red, looks with gigantic flashing eyes at the bonfire made by the townspeople, where the winter witch is consumed in the flames.

Disneyel

Every clock on the wall here is exactly ten minutes fast, as if they wanted to confuse someone who has never been confused, or to be generous and give you a little extra time, or to let you know that the rules here are different, Ma'am, and please wait until you're called to the recovery room, there's a television here too. Two old men attached to high beds with transparent tubes and covered up to their chins and I are invited to join in some light jump-roping, on condition of course that we have a jump-rope handy, as we were told, class. One-two one-two, the rosy-cheeked girl jumps and smiles at us encouragingly so we don't lose heart. On another channel they're showing a trial where most of the witnesses died long ago. A white nurse flies along the corridor with the speed of a cartoon character and comes back with a sad boy in a wheelchair. Why did you create yellow children, Lord? Yellow and bald, as wise and weary as a shadow.

Come to slowly, Mother. There's nothing to see outside; it's just cold and gray, and a bitter merciless rain has been falling since morning. I brought you the Austrian Mozart chocolate balls you love and a wide shirt that hides. A green one. You'll probably call it a rag. And you have all the old pictures here, the ones Otek calls your solitaire: Menachem and Hannah on the balcony on Panorama Street, Otek nine years old dressed like a cowboy, and me at four, naked, wearing a hat, and with Michael at the beach in Bat-Galim. Michael is laughing at the camera or at you under his Rhett Butler mustache, and white orangeade foam breaks at his feet. And there's Father fixing the blue jalopy. His big hands are black and his glasses, in confusion, have slipped down his nose, which is also black. And you in a two-piece bathing suit, the daring bikini of those days: purple sunglasses, curls, and a huge coquettish smile under the colorful parasol that protects your sickly skin.

Just now a cleaning lady passed by in orthopedic shoes and a blue smock. She told me that the day before yesterday, when you came out of the anesthesia, she tried to feed you a little chicken soup. You tasted it and spat it out and said, Meat. How could I have forgotten to tell them? How could I have forgotten Friday nights in Grandma and Grandpa's old apartment on Hadar? Monsters of the dark rose up from every corner. Their eyes the flames of Sabbath candles. When somebody remembered to turn on the light, after an eternal darkness, the monsters changed into dust covers, superfluous things that no one sees anymore, except maybe you. Father eats chicken soup with noodles and the neck and the feet, each foot with four little rough yellowish toes, and then a drumstick and giblets, while you stare stubbornly and your fork clicks in the three-egg omelet like an artificial arm. The omelet appears on your special plate every Friday, and you put one greasy strip of it after another into your mouth until the plate is empty. Only then do we get the fruit salad. I came and gave you the plastic cup with lukewarm tea, and your lips pursed with offense, and I took you to the bathroom and folded the toilet paper and picked up and tied the faded pajama pants yellow as leaves, and I flushed like a nurse, my eyes averted from your pale flesh, and my heart ached. But on Saturday afternoon, after the sea when Father took me to his blue depths and taught me to swim and not be afraid of the mountainous waves, we would bathe and dress nicely. I had black patent leather shoes we bought once, before Michael came, remember? And we walked along the Panorama, and Hannah waited for us on the balcony, always smiling, watering her plants with a little purple sprinkling can, and you could smell her butter cookies from the sidewalk.

First we drank tea in view of the mountain and the bay below. You always said that wearing blue with green showed a deplorable lack of taste, but from the Becker family balcony, when Hannah poured English tea from the English china pot as thin and upright as herself into little cups wreathed with flowers and offered cookies in her fragile voice, the green of the mountain and the blue of the bay went together marvelously. You and Hannah, whose silver hair was pulled into a tight bun, quietly recalled your mother. Hannah had been her best friend back in the teachers' college, and on the anniversary of her death, between Purim and the Passover break, Hannah and Menachem would come to our house after the cemetery along with all your aunts and uncles from Rehovot and Rishon Le-Zion and Petakh Tikvah. Otek and I would wait all year for that day, because there were presents and cakes and Hannah's cookies, and Aunt Naomi, the divorcée from Tel Aviv, would bring bags of imported candy, as if it were a birthday. That was one of the two times in the year when you climbed on a chair and carefully brought down from the high cabinet in the hall the set of dishes that was exactly like the set at Hannah and Menachem's house, because they gave it to you for your wedding. And everyone made the cups clink and ring, and they ate the cakes with small polite forks, and talked loud, all at the same time, about the children who were getting married and the grandchildren who were being born, and after a few years about the diseases that were starting: diabetes, ulcers, high blood pressure. About Uncle Bezalel, who was in the hospital with cancer, a word they said with a special pleasure and quietly-timidly, the way schoolchildren say fart. And as they got older they ate more little cheese sandwiches and less cake, then not all of them came, and those who did talked about them and about trips abroad, their own trips and others'. Then after a few hours they started yawning without covering their mouths, like cats, and I would bet on which one yawned next. They also brought Grandpa from the old age home, where I once saw a silent black-and-white movie with Charlie Chaplin, and all the old people quacked with toothless laughter. Each time he came, Grandpa had fewer words, and once he wanted to ask if this was cherry cake, and he tried hard to remember but finally gave up and said kirschen, and anyway it was straw-berry cake. Every time he lost a word he would fold his arms in his old brown sweater and sink into the armchair until his shriv-eled body almost vanished and only his bird's face showed above the armrest. And he would look around with furious amazement and suspicion and say in his thin voice, What am I doing here, I'm from yesterday's world. Once he told me a secret, that a famous professor in America had invented a medicine against forgetting, and with a shaking hand he gave me the napkin for the cake and told me to take a pencil and write a letter on it to the professor, saying that he Grandpa was willing to come to America and be a guinea pig for the new medicine. And you heard, and said to him, Why are you confusing the child, and Grandpa exploded and threatened you with a bony finger, My uncle Reb Leyb Green died at the age of ninety-six and his mind was perfectly clear. I drank my tea and milk very carefully so nothing would break, and I thought to myself that the set of dishes would stay down now, because Michael was coming soon, as every year at the beginning of the Passover break, a few days after Grandma's Yahrzeit, but once I wasn't careful enough and the cup slipped away from me and broke in two and all the tea spilled on my feet and on the carpet and the floor, and you yelled, Be careful, what are you doing. You blushed, and I worked hard not to cry while Hannah wiped my feet with a napkin and said, I'll give you one of mine, but you said quietly, It doesn't matter anymore, and Hannah, sad and proud, told again about her son in America. The sweet, serious smoke from Menachem's pipe mingled with the perfumes and the cookies and the English tea and the pine tar of summer's end, and I took another cookie, which melted in my mouth too fast, and tried to pay attention. Otek was in the living room listening to the Saturday football game on the radio, and every now and then he would come to the balcony to take some goodies, and Father drank black coffee and ate black grapes and was silent.

Sometimes, when there was a war or elections, you all talked about the Political Situation. Then Menachem would put his arm through yours and lead you to the studio, and I followed quietly, and he would show you his new roofs and skies and explain and point with his finger, and you would nod, and I remained awhile to look and smell all the paints and the special materials artists have. Recently, when Naomi asked you for one of his three paintings in the house, roofs-and-sky in brown and pink from '54, in blue-green and gray from '64, and in orange-yellow and black from '74, and said, Maybe you'll give me one for the new apartment, they're all the same anyway, you looked at her in amazement and said, What are you talking about. But then you said, Once Menachem tried to paint carnations in a vase but it didn't work, and you laughed.

When you said goodbye at the door, it always took a long time, because that's when they really started talking, and they said again how pretty you were and how terrific you looked, while I danced in my black patent leather shoes and white skirt on the red linoleum, which reflected Hannah's whole kitchen, and Menachem applauded and cried, That's how Shirley Temple dances.

On the way home you said, Vacation's over, tomorrow you go back to school. Otek said, Yuck, and Father said again how good the show was at the end of the last school year and how I had recited that poem so fine, he didn't remember which one, and he said, When you grow up you'll be a radio announcer. And you said, She'll be whatever she wants to be. I remembered that I had been sick then and my teacher Nehama came to my house especially to give me the book by Miriam Yalan-Shtekelis, which I didn't need because I already had it. She told me to learn the poem by heart for the show at the end of the school year, I waited and wept because Michael wasn't coming. I was the only one who had such a long poem to recite, but I did it well because I thought about your Michael. What will I do if one day he really doesn't come, I thought, and almost wept, and everybody applauded. But he always came in the first days of the Passover break and also after summer vacation, when school started, when I would ask you for five lire and go to Max's store, Max with his good smile and a number next to his rolled-up sleeve. There was always a long line there and a crowd, and I would buy ten notebooks and plastic wrappers and bookcovers and felt-tip pens and pencils and a pencil sharpener and an eraser that smelled and a pad of shiny and sticky colored paper and some paste, and by the time I left the store it would be almost dark, chilly, and when I came back home you were in the kitchen making dinner, and afterward I asked you to wrap my books for me, but Father, who was listening to the radio, said, Quiet the news is on. I knew that in a few days you would tell me, Today we're going down to Hadar, and you would say to Father who was just coming home from work, We're going to buy something for the holidays or for the change of season. We'd take a cab and get off at Nordau and go to the corner of Herzl and Balfour and go across the tunnel under the street, where the fat old man in the wrinkled suit lived, playing sad melodies on his violin, and you would toss ten or twenty agorot and sometimes even half a lira into his open violin case lined with red velvet, where there was always a lot of money. We'd come out on the other side, right into the store of the two old German Jews who were both called Mrs. Müller because they were sisters, but they seemed like twins, both having the same silver bun as Hannah and glasses that hung on a string on their droopy breasts and hands covered with big brown freckles, and long red fingernails and a lot of rings, and neither had a husband. You asked if they had something new for the change of season, and the Müller sisters said, For a beautiful woman like you we have everything. You went behind a curtain and tried on knits and satin blouses and long rustling silk skirts in shades of green that matched your eyes, and purple which you especially loved. Yellow clothes you never tried on, and blue ones hardly at all. My job was to stand by the curtain and hand you a bigger or smaller size and tell you which was prettier, because you always hesitated and couldn't make up your mind. The Müller sisters said, On a beautiful woman like you everything is beautiful, and they took a new and splendid silk or velvet dress out of some hidden place, and you tried it on and looked in the mirror and blushed and your eyes shone. They stood on either side of you and also looked in the mirror, with their tiny smiles and tiny gray eyes flashing like pinheads, and you said, I'll take it. Then we would go buy something for me, but every time in a different store, and you always knew right away what suited me, and you paid and that was it. But I wanted to choose by myself, because Michael always noticed every detail, and once in the spring I chose by myself a white sailor suit and black patent leather shoes and Michael picked me up high in the air and called me his little sailor girl. After shopping, we went to Café Atara, where there's a MacDavid's now, and we drank iced coffee with ice cream and ate cream cake. A yellow-haired woman was always sitting there, with powder on her face and her lips painted like a little red butterfly, and she waved to me and smiled, and she had a gold tooth, but you whispered, Don't talk to her, and I said, Why, and you said, When we get home you can help me take the set of dishes down from the cabinet.

Here comes Dr. Morgenstern down the long corridor, a skeleton in a white lab coat. He is unfocused and annoyed, like a bus driver peering through a steamy windshield on a rainy day, his passengers a nuisance, and he says the operation was a success and there's hope, but it'll be a few more hours before they bring you out of the recovery room, so I should go and come back later or even tomorrow morning. But I'm comfortable here. The old men in their high-tech beds have been removed to wait somewhere else, and there are cartoons on the television now. Meanwhile, without realizing it, I've eaten more than half the Mozart chocolate balls. You would eat one each night before you went to bed, like medicine, making them last, and I had to ask special permission to take one, because Michael brought them to you from Austria in red tin boxes with gold writing, but it took me a minute to gobble up the Austrian cat tongues he brought me. In Israel the only cat tongues were made by Lieber, with the advertisement On every tongue Lieber's a song, which we saw at the Armon movie house at the matinée, between the black-and-white newsreel about Nasser dying and the feature Gone With the Wind. You cried when Scarlett O'Hara, wearing a splendid green velvet dress she made for a party out of a curtain because she was poor, brought her cherry-red lips to Rhett Butler but he didn't kiss them, and the whole audience laughed, and the second time you cried was at the end, on the stairs. Michael climbed the stairs now in his squeaky new shoes and white safari suit, and I waited for him at the door while you gave yourself a quick spray with the narcissus perfume he once brought you, and Michael picked me up high in the air and kissed my cheek with his prickly mustache and his sharp good smell, and said, How gorgeous you've grown, or sometimes, My little sailor girl. Then he hugged you and whispered a secret in your ear, and you laughed and said, Fool, and suddenly you were young, as in the pictures of you from school and the army and your wedding, which I have here with me to give you when you wake up.

Father and Otek had long ago gone to the field to play soccer, so there was only us with the tea and the cheesecake you baked once a year. The other time in the year there was Apfelstrudel, which is better than what they have in Austria, said Michael, and he drank the pale tea and ate only a teensy piece of cake because he didn't want to get fat. Then he opened his big case with stickers from all kinds of countries in all kinds of languages, and took out a green bottle of French champagne, and choco-lates, and presents that were better each time, a big soft panda, a watch with a picture of Mickey Mouse, a grown-up doll that could talk in German and had her own suitcase filled with dif-ferent clothes so she could be a doctor, a stewardess, or a model, and he brought you perfume and earrings with green stones that sparkled like eyes, and an electric hairdryer. Then he took out

of his case a brown cardboard folder with the word Disneyel on
it, a combination of Disney and Israel, and of Michael too, and
he opened the folder and spread it out on the table, and a few
years later on the sofa too, and after a few more years on the
carpet too, pages and pages of calculations, columns of numbers
thin and thick, and pictures of the real Disneyland in America,
with a giant Mickey Mouse and Donald Duck, which I knew
only from birthday party movies because there weren't televisions
in many houses yet and not in ours. You kept one of the Mickey
Mouse pictures, of Michael photographed with him, and maybe
that's the joker in your solitaire deck of picture cards. There
were also color drawings of roller coasters and Ferris wheels,
because Michael had bought a used one in Germany, and cable
cars, the people next to them like tiny ants. And there were
horror tunnels and intricate car tracks and a hall of mirrors which
made you look sometimes thin and sometimes fat, sometimes
pretty and sometimes ugly, sometimes young and sometimes old,
and a pond with white sailboats and swans, and a big café on
the banks of the pond, white garden chairs with high carved
backs and round tables and colorful windowpanes and an orchestra and a dance floor, and Michael had even drawn bowls
of ice cream on the tables. Crawling across the carpet, he'd talk
fast and loud about all the perfect things he was going to invent,
and about financial obstacles and other obstacles he came up
against in Vienna, America, Israel, keeping him from putting a
Disneyel in the Galilee or the Negev, and about some very rich
Jew who was interested in the project and had promised to get
him a meeting with Walt Disney himself. Then Michael lay on
his back panting between the Ferris wheel and the pond, and
you smiled smug little smiles to yourself, but I jumped on him
to have my own private Disneyel in the meantime, and Michael
grabbed my hands and put his feet-in-white-socks on my stomach

and lifted me high and said, Air-o-plane. I asked if he could do the air-o-plane with you too, and he did, and you flew in the air and laughed and laughed, but then you fell on top of him and your new dress wrinkled up and one green earring fell into the pond, and Otek and Father came back with the soccer ball. They were wearing blue-jean shorts with blotches of sweat on their shirts, and you and Michael stood up, and you quietly straightened your dress and picked the earring off the carpet, and also took the other earring off your ear. Michael quickly put on his shoes and smoothed down his hair, which had got messy, and he shook Father's hand. Father said, How are you, and Michael said, Fine and you, and tapped Otek on the shoulder and said, Hi there big boy, and gave him a water pistol or something like that, then said he had to go because people were waiting for him.

After Michael left, I would sit at the window for hours watching the rain and thinking about him and the imaginary land he would build and be king of, and you would be queen and I the little princess. Sometimes I couldn't control myself anymore and I would ask you if they'd started building it yet, and Father would laugh, then you would get mad at him and say, It can't be done in winter, it's too cold in the Galilee. Then Purim came, and Otek dressed up as a cowboy again, with the water pistol Michael gave him, which looked like a real gun, and I was a princess. Then Grandma's Yahrzeit came, with Hannah's cookies, and the yawning championship of the aunts and uncles, where the losers were the ones whose heads dropped onto their chests like broken dolls, and the imported candy of Aunt Naomi who was a divorcée because her husband hit her once. She had a child bigger than Otek, almost bar mitzvah age, and every time I saw her, I thought, If Father and Mother get divorced, which one will I choose. Grandpa had few words now and would ask for things in a very thin voice that poked like the finger he shook from his armchair when he said trembling with anger, My uncle Reb Leyb Green died at the age of ninety-six perfectly lucid.

On one of the first days of the Passover break, a hot day, ninety-five degrees they said on the radio, I heard a horn downstairs and ran to the balcony. Michael was standing next to an enormous white car, smoking a cigarette and honking the horn and shouting, Come to the beach. We got into our bathing suits quickly and ran down, just you and I, because Father was at work and on school vacations he took Otek along to help him. In the car, I sat in the back and Michael sang in a thick voice, Put your head on my shoulder, and every time he came to that line you put your head on his shoulder and the two of you burst out laughing, and then you harmonized, All you need is love, love is all you need, which was all you heard on the radio the last week, and when we got to Bat-Galim, we sat at the edge of the water but didn't go in because Michael couldn't swim. Instead he drew his Disneyel with his finger on the wet sand and added round lottery stands and target shooting stands, and said that if you hit the black heart of the plaster woman right in the middle you'd get a plane ticket around the world, and if you didn't win you could go into the ball-shaped movie theater, which Michael drew, explaining that the film is projected in a circle and you stand in the middle and feel that everything is really happening. A big wave came and the white foam erased all our drawings, and I said to Michael, Winter's over now. And he said, What. I asked, When are they going to start building. He said, You can't do it in the summer, it's too hot in the Negev. And I asked, Is that really so or just an ell-eye-ee. And he said, What. And I said, Disneyel-eye-ee. And he said, What are you talking about, and looked at a white sailboat gliding teasingly slow along the breakwater. Then you said, Come on let's make a sandcastle, and we dug a hole which filled with water, and took wet sand out of it, and our hands touched in the hole, my little hand and your big hand and Michael's. We made a sandcastle, and I decorated it with shells and stuck my ice-cream stick on the top. Then we went to buy falafel, and there was also corn-on-the-cob, but you said that was too much, and when we went back our castle was almost completely destroyed, but you two didn't care. On the way home, you didn't sing, so I recited the poem, Michael, for you, and then the one about the Redhead, which I remembered, Many are the colors you have my Lord, blue you spread over the skies, and for my mother green eyes, the whole poem, and Michael said, That's terrific, and he said, Every time I hear those poems, I want to cry like a baby. You looked out the window and said nothing. Michael let us out, and we waved to him until he vanished around the corner, and we went upstairs, and even before you took a shower you climbed on a chair and put the set of dishes back in the hall cabinet.

Dr. Morgenstern, Dr. Morgenstern, please come to the office, telephone. I've been here since noon, and the bored clock on the wall shows 5:15, which means 5:05. I won't even bother to look at my Swatch Watch to see if that's right because what difference does it make, with you asleep there or coming to slowly like light opening: Yes, ma'am, you're still alive. Behind me is a procession of metal carts with dinners for patients, an omelet and a tomato and yogurt and tea in blue plastic dishes. I stand at the window watching the darkness that will come soon and the rain that hasn't let up for a minute, as on that winter afternoon right after Hanukah when you suddenly said, We're going down to Hadar today. I looked at you without understanding, so you said again, We're going down to Hadar today, and at five o'clock we took an umbrella and went out. The wind with a long whistle swept us up like Mary Poppins to a taxi, and then from the taxi all the way to the corner of Herzl and Balfour. We passed through the violinist's tunnel, and there was a gust and water streamed inside. He wasn't playing, he was sleeping in his suit on his side on a torn blanket and hugging himself, and his violin lay next to him and the case was open and there were almost no coins in it. You took out a whole lira and put it on the red velvet, carefully so as not to wake him, then we came out at the store of the Müller sisters, and inside it was warm and comfortable. Mrs. Müller said, Will you have a cup of tea, and you asked, Is it ready, and the other Mrs. Müller said, For a beautiful woman like you everything is ready. She vanished for a moment and came back holding a hanger with a dress the green color of a French champagne bottle and embroidered with gold thread. You took it and went behind the curtain, then you came out and faced the mirror, and for a moment I couldn't breathe. The Müller sisters stood on either side of you and looked with their sparkling gray eyes and shook their heads and said it had to be shortened. They were already kneeling quickly on one knee, as if they were young girls, and put on their glasses, and hundreds of little pins sprouted from their shriveled mouths as they started folding the dress and sticking the pins into the green velvet, but you quickly tapped your foot and said, I'll take it as it is. The Müller sisters made strangled sounds of protest because they couldn't speak, until one of them took the pins out of her mouth and said, But Madam, and you said, I'll wear it with high heels. The Müller sisters stood up humbly and said, Bitte, and their four pinhead eyes shone more than ever. You paid, thanked them, and we went out into the darkness and the pouring rain. We didn't buy anything for me, and we didn't sit in Café Atara, though I knew exactly which cakes, cakes misty in the steam of the window, I wanted to order. Instead you gave me your hand and we went on walking, almost running, the lights flickering in the wet street, and we passed the big cigarette billboard which went on and off and on over the building on Herzl Street, where Grandpa rented out space, and where every year, on Independence Day, we watched the parade of dancers. Once big floats passed by with dolls of Golda Meir the Prime Minister and DeGaulle from the song Old DeGaulle has the biggest nose of all. But Grandpa sold the building because the old age home with Charlie Chaplin movies cost too much money. After the big synagogue we went into a shop I never noticed before, it was a fabric shop with sheets and towels and tablecloths arranged on shelves by color. You talked with the salesman, who was short and bald and wore glasses, and suddenly he came to me and said, How's the little girl, and I was amazed and said, Fine, and he said, My Shirley Temple doesn't recognize me. Then I saw it was Menachem, and I turned my head away, not wanting to talk to him, because what was he doing here and why was he wearing glasses and where were his paintings with roofs and his pipe with the smoke up to the sky? But he said, Never mind, on Saturday we'll be friends again. Meanwhile you selected a red tablecloth, and he wrapped it up for you. You opened your purse to pay, but he said again, Never mind, and you took out three ten-lira notes and said, Take it, but he said, You really don't need to, then he walked us to the door and said, See you Saturday, Hannah will bake cookies. He tried to pat my head but I didn't let him, and I was glad when we left, even though it was raining hard, and you waved to a taxi and we took it all the way home.

At school the next day I couldn't stop thinking about Menachem in his dark little shop, and through the window I watched the rain, which looked as if it was never going to stop, and at the gray sky and the red roofs in the ravine. I was cold, so I sat on my hands to warm them, and thought of what I would say

to Menachem tomorrow. The teacher, who wasn't Nehama anymore but Aviva, said, You're not paying attention today, so I
tried to listen to what she was saying about the evil Antiochus,
because even though Hanukah was over we hadn't got through
the whole lesson on the Maccabees. We went home at twelve,
as every Friday, ate lunch, and you and Father went to rest while
Otek and I played with the big radio in the living room and
changed stations. Otek found a broadcast of the world boxing
championship, which didn't interest me at all, so I went to your
room and saw as always your two knee-mountains covered with
a big down comforter. You were hiding behind them with the
weekend newspaper, which was on the other side of the mountain
and turning the sheets black. I crawled into the gully between
the two of you, Father and Mother, and took the weekend supplement and leafed through it. There was an interview on the
Political Situation with Ben-Gurion, who Dad always said was
a great man, but I didn't read it because it looked boring, and
there was an article on Eli Mayzels, who had a degenerative
muscle disease and his whole body was paralyzed, in a wheelchair,
it looked like a child's body, but he studied at the university,
just with his head, and even had a girlfriend, Tsippi, who wanted
to marry him, and he said in the interview that life was wonderful.
On the back page there was an article about fashion with pictures
of pretty women smiling. They had long-long legs and short-
short skirts called minis, and I asked, Why don't you wear a skirt
like that, and Father laughed and you looked at him a moment
and said, That's for young women. I decided that when I became
a young woman I would wear a mini. At four on the dot, you
got out of the warm bed and put on another sweater, even though
the rain had stopped and the sun was out and the mountain was
trimmed with gold in honor of sunset. You went to the kitchen

while Father dialed and told Grandma we couldn't come today because we had a guest for dinner, and he said, Good Shabbos and we'll see you. I was glad and thought, Good, now just the two of us will have a talk, but Father fell asleep as always with the pillow over his head. So I looked at his face, which without his glasses was like a blind bear, and I wondered if Michael was the dinner guest. I got up to ask you, and on the way saw the big table in the dining nook, which we almost never used, and it looked like the Christmas table I always imagined when I read The Little Match Girl. The red tablecloth we bought yesterday in Menachem's store was spread on it, and the set of dishes, little plates for appetizers and big plates for the main course and bowls for soup and bowls for dessert, and beside every plate a pink cloth napkin with shiny silverware on it, and a glass for the champagne, though Otek and I would have orangeade. In the middle of the table were two candlesticks with tall pink candles, transparent glass vases with red carnations and white ones like snow, and the little match girl blinked in amazement and felt she was dreaming, but finally decided it was real and Michael had to come.

Soon it will be so late, I'll ask them to set up a cot for me, because it would be crazy to go back to Haifa in this downpour and start looking for a hotel. They could let me stay in your room. The thought frightens me. I picture your mutilated body. It is a new moon that won't grow full anymore. No, I don't want to see you twisted in pain. Mama, I'm frightened. I turn the television on again, to calm myself down. On the news they're talking about traffic accidents caused by the weather, and about the budget, and an old man who came here in a wheelchair is shaking his head and whispering, Bastards. A late visitor, flir-tatious makeup, yellow hair, and a mouth painted like a little red butterfly, hurries by in black high heels, clip-clop down the corridor from the bedroom to the living room, while we sit and wait on the sofa like children in school after the bell rings.

First I changed my school sweater for something dressier, though I didn't have anything new, and Father and Otek showered and their hair was wet and combed to the side with a part, and they wore black pants and blue shirts and looked like Aunt Naomi's son Danny at his bar mitzvah a week before when we went to Tel Aviv especially for that. Then you appeared, green and washed and shining, like Mount Carmel at dusk after the rain. The green earrings on your ears, your neck and shoulders bare, soft, and a fresh smell from your wet hair held with gold combs. We all sat and waited, and Father said, So when is he supposed to come, and went on reading the afternoon paper, and Otek turned on the radio and just switched stations, Arabic and Sabbath singing, and you got nervous and said to him, Turn that off. I couldn't stop looking at you. After a while Otek kicked the table and said, I'm hungry, and Father said, So am I, and you said, In a little while. But you didn't do anything, you just sat in the armchair like a queen and looked at some distant point on one of Menachem's roofs, and I made another tour of the table to be sure nothing was missing, and nothing was missing, so I came back and sat down. At eight Father turned on the radio and said, Quiet the news is on, even though it was very quiet, and they told about a car that had turned over because of the weather and slippery roads, and I saw you gripping the arm of your chair tight. Father left the radio on, and there were nice Hebrew songs for the Sabbath, and I hummed along with them a little, and you said, Why don't you shut up. The radio again beeped and said, The Voice of Israel from Jerusalem Good Evening and Good Sabbath the time is nine o'clock this is the news by Moshe Hovav we begin with the headlines, then suddenly we heard a loud knock at the door, like kicking, and Father shouted, Who's there, and a voice said, Police. He ran to open it, and in the doorway stood Michael. All we saw of him was his face and mustache dripping rain and the huge grin of a boy who is wild but everybody loves him, and his long legs in white trousers and brown Italian shoes. Between his face and legs he held an enormous package wrapped in flowered paper and tied with a red ribbon, and he came inside and set it heavily on the carpet and said, I got stuck because of that accident, and he said to me, Open it. I stood and waited until everybody was watching me and then pulled the red ribbon and got snarled in the cellophane and lifted my face to him for help, but he was looking at you with shining eyes and you couldn't decide whether to smile and forgive him or not. At last I tore away the wrapping, and underneath was cardboard, and Michael helped me open it and inside I saw a lovely wooden box. Michael took it out of the cardboard, and it was a real television, brand new. Otek said, Hey fantastic now we have a television too, and Father came up and leaned over and asked, What brand is it, but he didn't look at Michael, who said, It's Japanese and you can't believe the trouble they gave me at customs. Otek wanted to plug it in immediately but you said, Later first we'll eat, and Michael gave Otek the keys to his car so he could go down and get the bottle of champagne. We already had a shelf full of them in the cabinet because we never opened the ones Michael brought. You went into the kitchen and Michael followed you and said, Come on I'll help you, and Father sat alone at the table and waited. I followed you into the kitchen and saw the two of you mixing the salad and I said to Michael, Sit down, I'll help Mama. You and Michael looked at each other and Michael laughed and bent over to me and took my face in his hands and said seriously, Don't grow up too fast little girl. Then he went to sit with Father, and I heard one of them tapping his plate with his silverware. You ladled asparagus soup into the bowls and took the hot dishes out of the oven, eggplant stuffed with vegetables and peppers stuffed with rice and cheese and mushroom soufflé with sour cream, and I put everything carefully on the table, then you took a roast chicken out of the oven and I was amazed because we never ate meat at home, only at Grandma's. You held the pan at the very edge so your fingers wouldn't touch the chicken and you said, Put that next to your father, he can't do without his chicken on Friday. So I put it next to Father, and Otek came back with the champagne and we all sat at the table. Michael stood up and took the cork out of the green bottle and a little foam came out and he poured for you and Father and himself, and I said, I want some too, so he poured me a little too, and Otek was the only one who drank orangeade. Michael raised his glass and said, Lechaim and happy new year to all of us. I said, What are you talking about, this isn't Rosh Ha-Shana, and you explained that it was the Christian new year, which came right after the little match girl's Christmas, and Michael said, This is the new year for almost the whole world. We started eating, and Michael looked at the chicken from which Father took a drumstick, and said that the traditional food of the Christians today was turkey stuffed with prunes and nuts and raisins, and you said, He won't know the difference, and laughed because you'd had two glasses, and your eyes were bright with golden champagne bubbles, which made you very beautiful. Father held his drumstick and gnawed at it and sucked the bones noisily, and Michael ate a lot and said everything was delicious, and it really was delicious, maybe because of the set of dishes which reflected the flickering candles as if they were happy eyes. He told about the deals he was doing with Japan, importing televisions and other electronic instruments to Europe, and he

said how funny the Japanese were, and he got up from the table
and squinched up his eyes into two narrow slits and imitated a
Japanese, bowing all the time and saying Hi, which is yes in
Japanese. You laughed and laughed, and turned red and started
coughing and champagne trickled from your eyes, but Father
didn't laugh at all. Michael said the Japanese had geishas, and
I asked, What's that, and he put his hands together and walked
with quick little steps like a woman and said that they used to
have extremely tiny feet because they were bound when the girls
were very young, and he said he was planning to import a few
geishas to Europe. But all through dinner he didn't say a word
about Disneyel, and I didn't ask him because suddenly it seemed
wrong to ask him. After dessert, which was hot chocolate cake
with vanilla ice cream, Michael lit a cigarette, and you told us
to go to bed, it was late, but Otek said, What about the television, and you said, Tomorrow, so he went to bed because he
was tired and not interested in anything, but I said, Just a little
longer, and Michael said, Let her stay up. You turned on the
radio, and there was dance music, and you looked at Michael
and Michael looked at you, and you went to Father and held
out your long white arm to him and said, Come let's dance, and
Father started to take it, but then you said, Wash your hands
first, and Father went to the bathroom so you and Michael
danced. He put his hand on the small of your green back and
you put your hand on his shoulder, and he held your other arm
by the elbow like a swan's neck in the palm of his hand, and
together you whirled around and around until the whole room
spun. Father came back with clean hands and danced with you
a little, but he was too heavy and couldn't spin around so the
two of you danced in place. You rested your face on his blue
shirt, and he lowered his head until his cheek touched your hair,
and I thought to myself, Remember this moment, keep this

picture very carefully in your memory. Then Michael swung me
up and we danced and spun on the carpet around the new television, and I laughed. You opened your misty eyes and told him,
Put the child to bed. And Michael carried me into my room and
put me on the bed but didn't turn on the light, there was a little
light coming from the living room, and he whispered, Pick up
your hands, and pulled the sweater over my head, so for a moment
it was completely dark and I couldn't see anything. He unbuttoned my blouse slowly and took it off, then took off my brown
shoes and my socks and undid my pants and pulled them down
one leg at a time and whispered, Where's your nightgown. I gave
it to him, and he put the warm flannel nightgown on me, and
his hands were cool. He tied all the ribbons on the sleeves and
at the neck, and said, Now lie down, and he hugged me and
gave me a long goodnight kiss in the dark, with his prickly
mustache and good smell, then he covered me with a blanket
and stood up and left, and went back to the living room. I
couldn't fall asleep, I didn't want to, so I listened to the music,
Put your head on my shoulder, but then it stopped and there
was talking, though I couldn't understand the words, as in a
movie run backward where the voices are all strange. But I did
catch a word or two when you said, It's been years now, and
either Father or Michael said—I never noticed how similar their
voices were—But I asked you, and you said, What could I do.
And someone else said, I can't take it anymore. And you said,
Mental cruelty. And another voice pleaded, Enough. Then you
laughed an awful laugh, or was it weeping, and I hid under the
blanket and stopped my ears. When I opened them, it was quiet.
Then you said, You decide. And Father said, Enough. You went
on talking very quietly and I couldn't understand a language
without words. You started crying or laughing again, someone
hit the table and shouted, You're a bastard, and the answer was,

Low class, but the first voice went on, Bastard, they should have put you in jail long ago, criminal, and someone else screamed, I could kill you. I shivered under my blanket and heard you stamp your feet, and there was another shout, Ilona what are you doing. A horrible crash, silence, and again that laugh of yours, and I shut my eyes and prayed hard that nothing happened to the new television. And then the front door slammed and shoes ran down the steps into the thunder and lightning outside.

The next morning I woke up, and the window was blue with sky. I got out of bed and went to the living room in my night-gown, but everything there was clean and neat. The table stood in the dining nook as brown and indifferent as usual, as if there hadn't been a fancy dinner last night. Otek had already plugged in the television and set up the antenna and was twirling the buttons even though there were no programs on yet. I went into the kitchen, where you were sitting eating breakfast, all the chicken Father didn't eat yesterday, you tore it into pieces and ate it with your hands, with big bites, and sucked the bones. Father was leaning on the refrigerator and begging, Enough Ilona, stop, but you didn't answer him, you were busy with the chicken. He left the kitchen and didn't look at me or say good morning, and I watched you for a while then asked, Michael. You lifted your eyes, which were hard and dry as bones, and said, your mouth glistening with fat, Michael isn't coming anymore. I shouted, That's not so, you're lying, and ran to my room and slammed the door, and hid under the blanket and stayed there all day. That Saturday we didn't go to Hannah and Menachem because you weren't well, and you threw up all afternoon. I was relieved, because now I didn't have to talk to Menachem about what happened in his shop on Thursday.

It's not comfortable on the cot between cold stiff disinfected sheets that smell white. The nurse on duty did her best, almost as if I were a patient, and I think she was sorry I wasn't. I should try to sleep a little. Not count the minutes in the dark. Not wonder what time it is. It's 12:25. It's 12:35. It's a quarter to, three minutes to. It's one o'clock. Time for lunch. During the meal, you were silent. Chewing and swallowing in silence. You'd look at your watch again and ask me what time it was, and I'd look at my little Mickey Mouse watch with two dials coming out of his black nose, the one Michael brought me and I wore it with a white plastic band and everybody in my class envied me, until one day I lost it, and I'd say, Twenty-five to two. Once a year, a few days after school started, a postcard would come. On one side, a color picture, every year from a different country. On the other side, a stamp, but only from Israel, and always the same sentence, Happy new year, a year of happiness and health to all, Michael. I would take the postcard out of the mailbox when I came home from school, put it cool and smooth against my cheek, smell the fragrance of abroad, then put it among the other letters and bills that had come, and give them to you before lunch. It was 12:30, but you didn't ask. Afterward, the postcard would vanish and I would never see it again.

After the first postcard, from Switzerland, with white mountains like vanilla ice-cream balls over Lac Lucerne and where swans looked like plastic toys in a bathtub, Ben-Gurion died. At school they talked about him all week, what a great man he was, and Father stopped sitting with us at dinner. We ate quietly with the television news in the background, he listening to it and reading the newspaper at the same time, and only after we were done did he come into the kitchen and eat an omelet out of the frying pan, quickly, standing up, because ever since that chicken you didn't bring meat into the house. And that year you started walking around in an old flannel bathrobe and your house slippers from room to room, a cigarette between your fingers, because you had started smoking, but outside you wore your pretty clothes, though they were out of style and we didn't go to the Müller sisters' store even once. Next year the postcard came with a white airplane on a blue background, and Hawaii Five-O started on TV, and I loved the music with the tremendous waves that took my breath away, and when you asked me what time it was and Mickey Mouse said it was ten, you went to bed, and Otek and I forced ourselves to stay awake to see Steve McGrath, but Father didn't see him because he went out almost every night now and came back very late, after everybody was asleep, except me, since I couldn't fall asleep until I heard him come in and make his bed on the sofa in the living room. One day I came home from school and brought in the mail, which was only the electric bill, and went upstairs. You were in bed with a wet dishtowel over your forehead and eyes, and you were smoking a cigarette. I said, There's mail, and then saw that Father's socks-and-underwear drawer was open and empty. Then the neighbor twins from downstairs came up to see what a little girl looks like whose parents just got divorced, and they stood and stared at me but I didn't cry. Otek, my big brother who was in high school now, came and told them, My mother says you have to go because she doesn't allow anybody to come between two and four, so they left. The year we got the postcard from America with Popeye the Sailor Man, who was on television now much more than Mickey Mouse, Otek left home and went to live on a kibbutz in the Galilee, and Grandpa moved from his old age home to a nursing home, but you never took me there though I missed him. Once I went there myself on the bus after school, and walked through an empty garden, opened a heavy glass door, and entered a stink of urine and chicken soup. Breathing as little as possible, I looked for Grandpa among the old people at the tables trying to bring their shaking hands to their mouths without spilling anything, but he wasn't there. I went up to the second floor, where old people were lying, brown and creased like paper bags, plastic tubes coming out of them, and they sighed consolation to themselves in a soul language without words, or maybe they were arguing with God about their lives, or just watching the high white ceiling, the last image, like a movie screen when the film is over and the projector hasn't been turned off yet. I went from bed to bed looking for Grandpa among the bird-faces that were all alike. I stopped at one bed, but when the person opened his eyes, they were brown, and I saw it was somebody else. I went to one of the nurses and asked, Where is Aaron Green please. She pointed to an old man sitting in a wheelchair and said, There next to the door, so I went to him, and he was singing in a squeaky voice, and drumming on the arm of the chair with a blind animal hand, and he didn't recognize me, because it wasn't Grandpa. I went to the fat nurse with glasses behind the brown desk and asked, Where is Aaron Green please, he's my grandpa. She opened a thick notebook with a black cardboard binding and said, Aaron Green oh he died. I asked, When, and she said she thought it was yesterday but wasn't sure. She leafed more through the notebook, which wasn't very neat, and stopped and said, Aaron Green, no, I'm sorry, he hasn't died. So where is he, I whispered. She shouted to a nurse at the other end of the corridor, You remember Green the one with the—and said something in hospital language I didn't under-stand. The other nurse shouted back, That one, yes, they trans-ferred him this morning to Rambam Hospital, critical condition, coma, want a cup of tea, and my nurse shouted, Yes thanks, and to me she said, He's not here, honey, you can try at Rambam. I ran down the stairs and ran home, but didn't go to Rambam and didn't tell you, and now you have two Yahrzeits a year, two candles on the television set a month apart. Hannah and Men-

achem and your aunts and uncles from Rehovot and Rishon Le-
Zion and Petakh Tikvah who are still alive no longer come to
our house after they go to the cemetery perhaps because the
special tea set is no longer there.

The year we got the Versailles Palace, its turrets stabbing
the pale sky, you sent me to Aunt Naomi in Tel Aviv for the
vacation so you could rest, and I was glad because she kept Cokes
in her refrigerator and not just orangeade, and she had books I
hadn't read yet, Heidi and Little Women in a red binding. I
loved Jo especially, who married the German professor in the
end. There were also little shabby paperbacks, which belonged
to her former husband, with stories about the camp commander
who undressed the pretty female prisoner and made her go on
all fours in the snow and whipped her. At night, before I went
to sleep, I would open Little Women, but inside it I had one of
those paperbacks and read it with horror and burning curiosity,
but on Wednesday nights I didn't read, because Ironside was on
television. In the morning, when I got out of bed and went down
to the avenue shaded with big trees that dropped round black
fruit that spotted the sidewalk, I would remember how when I
was little and still had patent leather shoes, I was careful not to
step on the cracks. I was relieved to get back to Haifa, because
the sidewalks there don't have cracks between the squares and
you don't have to be afraid of the darkness beneath, the restless
darkness which always looks for openings to crawl into our world,
the world of light.

The year of the yellow lion family from the safari in Nigeria,
I started adding up the numbers on bus tickets and subtracting
the number of letters of the alphabet and the number of the bus,
route 23 to school and route 19 to Scouts, and calculating complicated Gematriya I would get the first letter of the name of the
man I would marry. One night, when I came home from Scouts

with a husband whose name started with M, Hannah and Menachem visited us because we almost never visited them since you
weren't strong enough, and Menachem gave you his last roofs-
and-sky because a few days later he fell down in his little shop
on Herzl Street and died among the colored fabrics. Hannah
buried him and went to her son in America, taking with her all
the cookies in the world.

The year we got the dark Brazilian woman with laughing
breasts but a regular Israeli stamp stuck on the back of it, you'd
get up from your afternoon nap and ask, What time is it, and
I'd say, Four. Then you'd take bundles of old photographs out
of the drawer that once held Father's underwear and sit in the
living room and arrange them by events and dates, and rearrange
them by the people in them, and then rearrange them again,
Grandpa and Grandma, Menachem and Hannah, Michael and
Father, and Otek and I and you yourself, and there were black
lines under your pretty green eyes, like dusty pines at the end of
summer, and your lips pulled in, from dragging on cigarettes,
and the curling smoke turned your hair gray as all of us smiled
at you. Otek came from the kibbutz on Saturday sometimes, and
held you to his broad chest, and you rested your face on his blue
shirt, and he lowered his head until his cheek with black bristles
touched your hair, and he would say in his rusty voice that
sounded like the machines he used in the carpenter's shop,
You've been playing solitaire with the family pictures again. Then
you would put the king, queen, joker, and all of them back in
their brown paper bag and make him coffee in the big china cup
the two of us once bought you for your birthday with Best Mother
written on it. Otek drank the coffee in big gulps and stayed until
the evening, watching Archie Bunker with us, and after the
weekly sports show he went back to his kibbutz. One Saturday

night, after he left, I opened the newspaper I hadn't yet finished and read that Eli Mayzels died at the age of twenty-nine.

Two years ago I came to you straight from work, brought in the mail, a card that showed a Japanese woman kneeling in the traditional costume of a geisha, and a jar too with a branch of cherry blossoms, and on the other side it said, A healthy and happy new year. I thought, Maybe we should worry about Michael, and laughed to myself. By then you weren't eating and I'd say, Go to the doctor, and you'd say, All right, but you didn't go, and you didn't sleep at night. When I went upstairs I thought, Maybe if I hadn't given you the postcards all those years everything would have been different. You lay in bed, and I put the mail next to you, and you asked, What time is it, and I said, Quarter to three, and that was the last postcard from Michael.

On one of those nights when Alexis threw Krystle off the horse and Blake was out of his mind with worry, you became unconscious. Soon they'll make the morning official here, long before the sun comes up, and a procession of metal carts will pass with the rumble of dishes and liquids and thermometers in cold corridors, in cold neon light. And I'll go into the room quietly, dreading and regretting. I'll search for your face always smiling in my memory, smiling as in the picture of you at Bat-Galim beach. And there you are, you who came back to me from great distances. On the nightstand by your bed I'll put the new green blouse and the Mozart chocolates, those that are left, and the photographs, and I'll hold your hand, which will be warm, or cool as it was in the winter when we used to run down Herzl Street. And I'll kiss you, and say, Mother. And you'll ask me, What time is it. And I'll answer you, 6:15 in the morning. And maybe we'll be able to hear the brittle thunder and the soft rain descending on the world as solace.

Closing the Sea

The bus to Tel Aviv stopped at Carmel Center in Haifa, swallowed up Ilana and three other passengers, and continued on its way. Only the girl in the pink bikini stayed behind at the bus stop, beautiful and smiling forever. Or smiling until somebody blackened one of her teeth or gave her a mustache, thought Ilana. She paid the driver and looked around quickly, afraid of meeting someone who knew her. After she got her change, she made her way between the packages and bags, and took a seat in the next to last row on the right, by the window, so that when they came down from the mountain and turned she'd be able to see the sea. As usual, she put her old brown purse on the seat beside her to discourage people from sitting there, then changed her mind and put it on her lap, but no one sat beside her anyway. Still she clutched the purse to her stomach and looked out, and her thin pale fingers with short nails unconsciously opened and closed the zipper.

The bus sped down the steep road to the sea, passed the rest home with its mammoth lawns and colorful chaise longues among pines, then Hotel Ben-Yehuda, before the curve where you could see the whole sea suddenly spread out below you, as if it hadn't been there all along. She recognized the tower of yellow hair three seats in front of her, Ronit's mother, and said to herself, Oh dear, why didn't I see her before. She certainly saw me and will tell the principal. When Ilana spoke to the principal on the phone an hour ago, he sounded suspicious, though this was the first time in seven years she had missed a day of work, but maybe that was why. Flu, two weeks before the summer vacation, asked Abraham, and she herself didn't know where she had got the nerve to call the school, which now was no school but an espionage agency with the most sophisticated lie detectors which even over the phone could tell you were lying. Never, in all her thirty years, thirty-one years next month, had she said a thing that wasn't true. Yet she dialed with numb fingers and a stomach full of rocks and spoke to Shoshana, the secretary, who said with annoyed impatience, Get well, and she spoke to Abraham, who grumbled that he didn't have a substitute. He also told her gravely that she would be missing a lecture by the deputy director of the city's Department of Education on the problem of integration, held in the gym after fifth period. Then finally he had said, in an unpleasantly intimate tone, Well, stay in bed, Ilana, and get better. So she was free, and she felt free as she watched the gold dust spilling on a slant through the slits of the shutters and melting into a giant coin on the floor. She pulled the thin blanket over her head, as she used to do on vacation mornings when she was a child, and curled up into a blind coil of pleasantness until she couldn't contain herself any longer and got up, washed, put on her dress with the big-flower print and thin shoulder ruffles, and looked in the mirror. She wondered how she would look to Tami, whom she hadn't seen for more than two and a half years, because Tami had been in Los Angeles with her husband Joel, and when she came back, she immediately started working on a series of ads and then on rehearsals for a new play. Hearing her voice in Hebrew and English on the answering machine, Ilana would say almost in a whisper, This is Ilana, or, Ilana called. After a few weeks, she stopped leaving messages because Tami was obviously too busy and couldn't return her calls. This morning, when Ilana called early, even before she talked to the school, she woke her up, but Tami seemed glad to hear her and said in a sleepy voice that she'd be at the theater all day but Ilana could come late in the afternoon, and they agreed on five. Ilana smiled at the face in the mirror and said to herself, You haven't changed a bit all these years. She saw a new sparkle in the big brown eyes behind the thick lenses of her glasses, and her usually pale cheeks were flushed. Her lips weren't cracked today, and her hair looked fuller. Suddenly she was satisfied with this skinny body with matchstick legs and barely distinguishable breasts, because she remembered how Tami would look at her enviously when they were twelve and standing in ponytails and pink leotards before the wall mirror in the ballet studio of Madame Valentina Archipova Grossman. Archipova had been a prima ballerina in Moscow in the thirties, until she married a Jew and moved with him to Haifa and opened the studio on thirty-seven Masada Street, which people said was a cover because she and her husband were really Russian spies. Once Ilana and Tami even followed them when they took their regular Friday afternoon walk. Archipova, upright and aristocratic in a long black satin dress, wore a high hat with a bunch of green grapes that hung coquettishly over her dark, pulled-back hair. In one hand, in a white kid glove, she held a yellow parasol, and her other arm was twined in the arm of her tall husband, who wore a black suit and top hat and held a black stick with a knob carved in the shape of a devil's head. They strode slowly, as if riding in a carriage, from their house on Hillel Street, turned onto UN Boulevard, and continued along the locked gates of the silent Bahai Gardens, their rhythmic footsteps the only sound on the steep slope deserted at that hour of silvery sky and excited colors over the sea. Then Archipova closed her parasol, and they were swallowed up in one of the side gates of the Persian Garden. At that same moment the golden dome of the prayer house grew dark, and the garden turned gloomy. Tami and Ilana pulled their heads out of the black fenceposts and ran to the end of the hill, and when they sat down on the green bench at the bus stop, Tami said, panting, That's it, now it's sure. They decided not to tell anyone because no one would believe them anyway. On Sunday afternoon, at the lesson, they exchanged glances during the plié and glissé and porte-de-bras, and Archipova yelled at them in her funny Hebrew over the piano music, and she waved the stick menacingly, the one with the devil's head. She had borrowed it from her spy husband to hit knees that wobbled or toes that refused to point. Ilana had the frightening thought that maybe Archipova knew that they knew, but on the way home, when they reached the Carmelite convent, Tami calmed her down and said, What are you talking about, that's impossible. Then she stretched and looked at her reflection in the train window as they flew through the dark tunnel, and said with a sigh, I'll never be a dancer, I'm too fat, you're lucky you're so thin. And Ilana looked furtively at Tami's breasts, which already showed through the pink leotard, two little plums with nipples, and at Tami's hips which were beginning to round, and she said nothing. Now she smiled in the mirror at that Tami, Tami the girl, at the saucy blue eyes and laughing black curls and lips always red as if she had just drunk raspberry juice. Ilana decided to put on a little makeup for her sake, even though makeup didn't really suit her and by five the colors would fade and she would have to put it on again. But she did everything as if Tami were standing there watching her.

She opened the shutter and stood barefoot on the balcony to smell the summer, which wafted to her through the pine branches, between the cones sticky with resin. Ilana knew how to use this stolen day of vacation. She should waste not a moment of it. First, breakfast. Today she would eat on the balcony, and have, instead of the usual slice of bread with jam and a cup of instant coffee before rushing off to her first class, an egg, fruit, some bread and cheese, and finally, with her coffee, a slice of the honey cake Mother gave her on Saturday despite her protests. Then she would take the express bus to Tel Aviv. It left Carmel Center at nine. She would sit in a café and watch the people. On your day off you didn't have to plan everything exactly, you could leave some room for surprises. Then she would go buy herself something pretty to wear for her date with Tami, maybe at Dizengoff Center, where she hadn't been yet and everyone said was terrific, just like America. She had been in Tel Aviv a year ago, for her twenty-three-year-old cousin's wedding, even though she didn't want to go, was afraid everyone would say, When's yours, but her parents begged her, so she went with them and no one made a remark. She had been in Tel Aviv also two and a half years ago, had planned to see Dizengoff Center, but it rained and they spent the evening at Tami's. They ate a good dinner Joel made and drank a lot of wine, and Tami talked with her usual breathless enthusiasm about the new play she was in, The Seagull by Chekhov. Ilana loved Chekhov and had taught a few of his stories in her class. Tami said she had got a small part, not the lead, Nina, and then she stood up suddenly and left the room.

The bus passed public beaches teeming with beach umbrellas and people and lifeguards' whistles and colorful surfboards, and

now they sailed along deserted beaches, which had only warning
signs and shrieking sharp-eyed gulls. The yellow tower of hair
in front of Ilana rocked slightly with the rolling of the bus until
it dropped to the right. Ilana remembered the postcard Tami had
sent her from Pisa on her way to the United States, and she
smiled and said to herself, Why are you so nervous. She raised
her eyes to the door, and Tami burst into the room wearing a
long blue dress with a crinoline, and her curls were pulled back
in an old-fashioned hairdo. Her eyes gleamed, her cheeks were
flushed, she was Nina, Nina just arrived in her carriage through
the snow, bursting into Kostya's room. Her words fluttered from
her mouth like wounded gulls, and her tears were real. Ilana felt
that some great magic was taking place before her eyes, as in the
school plays when Tami appeared on stage and was suddenly
someone else, and Ilana would sit in the first row, among the
parents and guests, and look up at her friend, whose clear voice
and shining face filled the big space of the gym. Ever since those
school plays, ever since Tami, in her blue school uniform, went
up to the lectern during recess and twisted her girl's face until
it looked like Miss Moses the nasty English teacher, and mim-
icked her grating voice and shook her sharp finger, calling one
of the students to the board, and everybody laughed and applauded, ever since then, Ilana saw her friend on the stage. Joel
hugged her, said she was a terrific actress and deserved the lead,
and Ilana wanted to say, Maybe you'll invite me to see the play
someday, but Tami wiped her tears on her husband's sleeve and
said, I'm exhausted, I'm going to bed. She made up the sofa in
the living room for Ilana, said goodnight, went into the other
room with Joel, closed the door. Ilana put on the flannel nightgown folded up in the little blue suitcase with the El Al tag, lay
down, and pulled the thick blanket over her head so she wouldn't
hear the sounds from their bedroom. But she didn't fall asleep

for a long time because of the gurgling of the rain in the gutter and the screams of the cats from the yard, which were like the screams of children in the playground at recess. Anat and Nurit twirl the jumprope, and she, the teacher, stands in line with the children. She wears a short pleated skirt and the blue school uniform, which is much too small on her. Soon it will be her turn to jump. I-la-na I-la-na, her students shout, and she hears the rhythmic slap of the rope on the burning concrete and knows her glasses will slip down her nose and her thin feet will betray her once again and once again she'll have to twirl the rope through all of recess until the palms of her hands are burning. Tami's there too, Tami the girl jumping and laughing at the grown-up Ilana, who has to twirl the rope for her and count to a hundred. Afterward, the bell for class, and Ilana takes her seat, the next to the last on the right, by the window. She has to bend over the desk, it's so low, and Miss Moses comes in with quick taps of her thin heels, stands at the lectern facing the class, raises her arm, showing the black hair of her armpits, curly and sticky with sweat, and points a long finger with red nailpolish at Ilana and says, You. Ilana goes to the board, clutching the anthology with Joyce's Eveline, which she read, recited, prepared carefully at home, and stands facing her students, who look at her with innocent eyes and wicked half-smiles. She leafs through the book with damp panicky fingers, begins reading aloud, and the English words are foreign to her. She tries to pronounce them a letter at a time, but only dull bleats come from her throat.

In the morning, Tami came out of the bedroom in a man's pajama top, the top three buttons open, exposing the soft cleft between her heavy breasts, and on her full white thighs Ilana imagined she saw red fingerprints. Disheveled and calm, humming to herself and smelling of ripe cheese, Tami fried eggs for them and set the table for a big breakfast. As they ate, dipping crusts into egg yolk, Ilana thought of telling Tami her dream, as when they were little girls sitting in the house they had built themselves with boards in the pine tree in Tami's yard. Basking in the sun like two cats, they would tell each other their dreams until Tami's mother came home from work and shouted, Get down from there, you'll kill yourselves. But Tami began talking about their plans to go to America, and Ilana was suddenly ashamed of her dream and said nothing. After the tree house they would go inside, stand in front of the huge mirror in the bathroom, which Ilana loved, because in her own house there was only a small mirror and it was high up in the door of the medicine chest and even on tiptoe she could barely see herself. They would make faces and put on Tami's mother's lipstick and eyeshadow. Tami drew thin black lines under their eyes and two long lines between their nose and mouth, and they scrunched up their cheeks and wrinkled their foreheads to see how they would look when they were old. Tami said, When we're old we'll look in the mirror in the old age home and remember this. And Ilana suddenly felt very happy, as if she had been promised something wonderful, and Tami smeared red lipstick on herself and said in a whisper, When I grow up I'll be an actress in the theater. Ilana wanted to ask now if Tami remembered, and she waited for an opportunity, perhaps when Tami began talking about the theater, but instead Tami talked about how their de-parture was being delayed by Joel's ex-wife because of her out-rageous financial demands. She hated him and she hated Tami even more because Tami had stolen Joel from her and their little daughter. Tami called her a witch, a black widow spider, and Ilana thought about the wife of Shmuel, her teacher at the university. Ilana would sit in the first row, sit in the light of his pleasant eyes, which were filled with wisdom, bitter irony, and the ability to love. When he read the cadences of Agnon, his warm voice would echo slowly in her chest and stomach as in a barrel of sweet rainwater. At dusk, when the autumn air on the heights of Mount Carmel was clear and cool and the women students pulled colorful sweaters out of their bags and wrapped themselves comfortably and hurried to hear the intelligent words of the lecturer, and when he inclined his head and smiled to himself like one who has his own way of seeing but so far no kindred soul to share it with, Ilana felt that she alone knew his thoughts, even though she could not put them into words. The sun, too, wrapped itself comfortably in a woolly cloud, only its bald yellow pate showing, and it tried its hand at watercolors over the whole soft silvery sky. Ilana knew great joy then, a shortness of breath, a rapid throbbing, and there was no room left in her for anything else.

One evening at the beginning of her third year, after class, when everyone left the room, Ilana went up to his desk. He was stuffing his books into his old brown briefcase and she stood before him, her fingers numb and her stomach fluttering with sharp-beaked birds, which she had felt so often those two years when during class she imagined confessing to him, and when she gazed at him forgetting to take notes and when she day-dreamed again on the bus as it groped in the dark to her parents' house, and again for hours when she couldn't sleep, seeing herself like the sports replays on television going up to his desk while he was stuffing his books away with his head bent, and saying, Shmuel. And he would raise his head, and his look, turned inward, would recognize her slowly and ignite into a smile for her, and she would repeat aloud the name that had been repeated inside her in a whisper for two years, Shmuel, I want to talk to you, maybe we can have a cup of coffee or go for a walk someday, when you have time. He looked at her as if he had known all along and said, Yes Ilana. Then he asked where she was going and offered her a ride. That very night, they sat in a small café downtown. She drank cocoa, holding the cup in both hands to warm them, and refused to have cake, despite his urging, and she saw the way he bent his broad body in the gray sweater and loudly sipped his tea with lemon from the thin cup he held so delicately in his big fingers. She had known for two years, imagining him, that that was exactly how he drank his tea. Outside, the first rain of the season began with light, hesitant drops, like the tapping of the toes of young dancers in their premiere performance. She said, It's raining. He looked at her affectionately and said he had a little time today because his wife was working late at the library, but he would have to go back to the university soon to pick her up. Ilana swallowed the sweet cocoa, which was quickly turning cold in her hands, and said nothing. He stroked her hair and dropped her off at her parents' house. After that, she looked for him during his office hours or in the cafeteria, and they would go for a walk in the grove near the university and talk mainly about the books he would lend her. One nice day at the beginning of winter, they went for a drive in his old car and passed the Druse villages of Daliat-El-Carmel and Usafiya. They stopped on the road near a large pine tree, and Shmuel took an army blanket out of the trunk and spread it between the rocks on the new wet grass that drank the sun with an excited hum, and Ilana lay on the blanket and he lay on her with his full weight, and moved and grunted like a bear, and grunted and sighed while she hugged his back in the gray sweater warm and damp with sweat. The sky was high and blue and the tree was a dense dark green and the sun was white and hard, hurting her eyes with colored needles as he grunted and sighed and she longed to absorb all his sighs into her. That was her first time. She was twenty-three and Shmuel almost twenty years older.

The absentminded smiling librarian, who always lost Ilana's

card and apologized and laughed and asked for her name again so she could make a new card, was his wife. They had two sons, one in high school, the other in grammar school. From that day on, Ilana went to the library frequently and sat where she could see and study her. The short hair exposing a soft vulnerable neck, the dimple that appeared in her left cheek when she smiled, the way she held her cigarette, the muscles in her legs when she climbed the stepladder. Ilana pictured her helping the younger son with his homework at the kitchen table, her straight long-fingered hand resting on his shoulder, or lying on the sofa in the living room watching television, her legs in sheer nylon stockings rubbing against one another on Shmuel's thighs as he sits next to her. Or giving him a cup of tea in his study, his broad back in the gray sweater bent over his great research project, Hebrew Literature of the Haskalah. He looks at her wearily and thanks her with his sweet smile, and in their bedroom she gets into bed, smokes and reads one of the books he will later lend Ilana, who will find ashes in it and a faint smell of handcream. Late at night, when he sits down beside her like a tired bear, they'll talk about everyday things, a broken washing machine, the mid-semester grades of the sons, the gift they have to buy for their parents' golden wedding anniversary, and the latest gossip about the dean, and the two of them will laugh under the blanket as they've laughed hundreds of times and will laugh hundreds of times more. At seven-thirty, when the library was about to close, Ilana would come to her, of all the librarians, and as she looked for the card, Ilana caught the faint smell of cigarettes and handcream and would take the book his wife gave her and whisper, Thanks, and flee from her blind smile in pain and shame.

After she graduated and began teaching at the school she once attended, Shmuel helped her put together a curriculum and gave her advice about what books to use. In their conversations

in cafés and on their walks on Mount Carmel they discussed how
to make children love literature, and sometimes he'd take the
army blanket from the trunk and spread it on the grass. The next
year, Ilana moved out of her parents' house and into a small
apartment on Bikurim Street. She furnished it cozily, sewed white
chiffon pillow covers and curtains, filled the balcony with plants,
and invited him. One afternoon he came holding a bouquet of
flowers. He was impressed by the apartment, which at that hour
was filled with the soft light of a summer evening, and sat with
her on the balcony overlooking the green ravine. He ate the
cookies she baked for him, drank a cup of tea with lemon, and
said that he and his family would be spending his sabbatical in
England where he hoped to finish his research on Haskalah literature. Tami, who was finishing acting school in Tel Aviv and
couldn't see Ilana until a few months later, consoled her on the
telephone and said it wasn't so terrible, she'd find someone else,
someone young and unmarried. But there was no one else for
her. At the end of that year, she sometimes thought she saw
him in the street, but when she approached, holding her breath,
he changed into a different person. One afternoon in early summer, she was amazed to see his wife downtown, in foreign clothes.
Ilana waited for a phone call that never came. Two weeks before
summer vacation, the war started and she saw in the newspaper
that his older son, the one he was so proud of and whom she
had never met, had been killed in Lebanon. She lay on her
double bed and wept, the newspaper scattered and despondent
at her feet, her arms helpless at her sides, and there was no
comfort. She wanted to see him but was afraid he wouldn't be
the one who answered the phone, afraid too that she wouldn't
know what to say to him. Three months later, she saw him with
his wife in a café. He was wearing the green vest she once knitted
him for his birthday. He had lied to his wife, told her his sister

sent it from America. Ilana fled, her glasses fogged like the classroom windows on rainy days, when students wrote their names and drew hearts on them with their fingers.

What are you thinking about, asked Tami, leafing through the newspaper, raising and lowering her eyebrows, exercises to relax the facial muscles. Nothing, said Ilana. Tami said there was no mention of her again in the review and she had to get dressed because they'd kill her if she was late. She disappeared into the shower and returned fresh and fragrant, curls wet and shining, and she wore red, black, yellow, all cotton. They left the house together. Tami put her cool smooth cheek next to Ilana's and kissed her with her raspberry mouth, and Ilana flinched a little, and Tami laughed her clear laugh and said, Bye Ilanchik, stay in touch. On the way back, in the bus, the heavy winter rain of Hanukah vacation fell, and Ilana said to herself that they hadn't really talked at all, and there had been so much to talk about, and this might be the last time they had together before Tami left.

Ilana looked out and saw that they had already passed Netanya, more than halfway to Tel Aviv. The driver turned up the radio so all the passengers could hear the ten o'clock news. The weather report said the temperature and humidity would rise, Tel Aviv thirty-three degrees Celsius, and everybody lifted their hands to check if the air conditioning was working even though they were almost there. In Herzliya, right before Tel Aviv, the yellow hair tower three seats in front of her stood up and Ronit's mother went to the door, but as she left the bus she aimed a sharp and cunning glance at Ilana, and the magical hours ahead exhaled and shriveled up inside her like old birthday balloons. Ilana went over the plan of the day again and resolved that nothing would ruin it for her. She'd go to Dizengoff Center, buy herself a fabulous dress, the kind you can find only in Tel Aviv, and sit in a café or restaurant, and all possibilities would be open till five. And then—a fragrant hug, a raspberry kiss, a clear laugh, and cups of coffee and excited tales into the night, as at scout camp in eighth grade, in the tent, in sleeping bags, with loud whispers and stifled laughs in the dark, and when she woke up the next day she discovered, with embarrassed joy, the blood of her first period.

The bus reached the Central Bus Station and opened its doors with a hiss of relief. Ilana got out, and the hot heavy air enveloped her in a sticky embrace, with the smells of urine and nutshells and frying oil and the shouts of fruit vendors and people selling cassettes, and noises too ornate, like the Oriental sweets she had never learned to like. At the base of the dirty green columns sat blind old men or amputees. For a moment they looked to her like ancient guards, who, in their cunning, knew that someday they would get up and take their deformities with them and crack the gates of the city, sealing the fate of all who were trapped inside. She walked quickly, trying not to look at the naked women whose enormous breasts sagged like empty parachutes and who spread their legs at the newspaper stands next to the information booth. On the way to bus No. 5, the one that went to Dizengoff Center, they told her at the booth, she suddenly felt very thirsty, but saw no stands around. She got on the bus, paid the fare, and stood at the back, because all the seats were taken. She peered out, trying to identify the streets, to read their names, Railroad Street, Allenby Street, Rothschild Boulevard. Her face was hot and her glasses kept sliding down her nose. She had to push them back up, again and again. When she got off the bus, her forehead was dripping sweat and her lips were parched, but she decided to put off drinking until she got to Dizengoff Center and could sit down comfortably in a café. She looked at her watch: five to eleven. Fourth period had started. Now she should be teaching the ninth grade. But she was here, in Tel Aviv, and still had six hours of surprises until her date. Her day off was only beginning.

As she waited at the curb, she saw a young man who was waving his arms at the cars zooming by, and shouting in a cracked and terrified voice, They're closing the sea, everybody out of the water, they're closing the sea. Then a dreary bitter laugh. People steered clear of him, stared gravely at private hidden points on the other side of the street, and rushed across when the light turned green. The young man, left standing there, went on waving his arms and shouting, They're closing the sea. Ilana saw that his mouth was crooked and his eyes were mute and his fingernails were black, and she crossed the street quickly and said to herself, A crazy boy, crazy. But something in her was nauseous and shaky, as if he had touched her and stained her dress.

Dizengoff Center sprawled in the sun like a lazy white concrete beast, the top part of its body on one side of the street and its front legs on the other, and its long neck and head in the sky. Ilana went in one of the entrances and was greeted by a puff of chilly air that dried her sweat, and she felt fresher. She was still very thirsty but thought she'd better buy the dress first so she'd know that was done and then could sit in a café in her new dress. She started walking along the shop windows. Her eyes, drawn to a stuffed bear or ceramic pitcher painted with flowers or some clothes she might buy, lagged behind her feet, which she forced to continue walking the paved, clean slope in this labyrinth of lights, smells, and music, because you couldn't stop, you had to keep moving, but she stopped at the next clothes store. In the window there was only a cream-colored matching skirt and blouse with gold buttons. On transparent wires, it looked as if it were floating in the air. Ilana knew she'd have to go inside to see what else they had. An elegant blond woman in a turquoise cotton dress with a cream-colored jacket was sitting at the counter in a cloud of narcissus cologne. Her blue eyes, like plastic buttons, surveyed Ilana with a rise of her thin eyebrow, and Ilana, embarrassed, wanted to leave, but the woman smiled pleasantly and said, Can I help you. May I look, asked Ilana, her frightened voice squeaking in her ears like new chalk on a blackboard. Yes, of course, said the shop owner, twisting her mouth as if she had bitten into something bad. She took a drag on the cigarette she held in her thin, many-ringed fingers and didn't look again at Ilana, who went to the rack of dresses and began going through them quickly, without seeing them, telling herself that in a while she could say goodbye, thank you and leave. May I help you, ma'am, a sudden voice over her shoulder said hoarsely. Ilana turned and saw a fat woman wearing a black miniskirt and shiny black pumps. Short hair dyed yellow, red lipstick smeared on her thick lips like tomato sauce. Ilana glanced at the counter, but the chair was empty, the shop owner had disappeared. No thanks, I'm just looking, Ilana whispered. The fat saleswoman said, What. I said I'm just looking, Ilana repeated, louder. The saleswoman reached out, pulled one of the hangers from the rack without looking, and ordered, Try this on. It was a tight black satin dress ending in a big balloon with hundreds of pleats the color of the saleswoman's lipstick. Ilana took the dress and went behind the curtain, told herself she would try it on to be polite, and then she'd go. She took off her clothes and tried to get into the dress without mixing up the openings. Her wet fingers couldn't button the shoulders. The fat saleswoman opened the curtain and said, I'll help you. She buttoned it with impatient fingers whose peeling fingernails were gnawed to the quick, then she dragged Ilana to a full-length mirror and said, Now isn't that terrific. Ilana looked at her thin white legs in sandals, chicken legs under the red cloth balloon, and said, I don't think so. But the saleswoman apparently didn't hear, and said, Look how beautiful that'll be with a belt. And five or six belts immediately appeared in her hand, a colorful cat-o'-nine-tails, and she put them on Ilana one after another, clasping her waist tightly. In the mirror, Ilana saw the shop owner, who had come back and was standing behind her. The elegant blonde assessed her, twisted her mouth into a smile, and said, Fantastic. The fat saleswoman said, I told her. With a body like yours everything will look terrific on you, and this black is just the right color, and you should wear black heels like mine. She put her thick foot forward and said, So you're taking it. Good. And immediately bent over and cut off the tag with the laundering instructions and price, and Ilana remembered that Tami had said to her long ago, Why don't you ever wear black. How much is it, she asked in a whisper. Not much, said the fat woman, there's a twenty-percent discount on the belt. The price of the dress was tremendous, almost half a month's salary. Ilana hesitated a moment, then told herself, In Tel Aviv you can't get something nice for less. As she was writing the check, the phone rang and the elegant blonde answered. They want the owner, she said to the fat woman, and handed her the receiver. Ilana looked at them in amazement. She had made a mistake, the fat woman was the shop owner. Ilana took the plastic bag in which they had put her old flowered dress, the name of the shop on it on both sides, in English and Hebrew, and said goodbye and thank you, but the owner was busy on the telephone and didn't hear, and only the blond saleswoman twisted her mouth at her in a smile and said, Enjoy it.

Ilana walked out of the shop with slow careful steps because the hem was so tight. People passed her quickly, men in suits, older women in blouses buttoned up to the neck and tied with a ribbon, and young girls in jeans and sneakers. She froze. Nobody was dressed as she was. Everyone was looking at her, their eyes like slivers of a shattered mirror. Her body a long black tube, and bony white legs with a red puff above them like a ridiculous clown's rear end in a target contest where nobody loses. Tears filled Ilana's eyes, as on the school playground during gym in third or fourth grade, when they ran around the field and one nasty girl behind her pulled her blue baggy sweat pants with the elastic waist and everyone saw her underpants. Stupid, she yelled at herself in a whisper, groping her way to the ladies' room to change her dress, stupid stupid. There was a line in the bathroom, so she washed her face. Her makeup was almost completely gone. She wiped her face with paper towels, dried her hands in the stream of hot air from the machine, and calmed herself: she'd go to the shop, return the ugly dress and get her money back, then sit in a café and finally have something to drink, and decide whether to look for other clothes or give up the idea altogether. She went into the bathroom, took off the belt and dress, folded the dress and put it in the bag, put on her flowered dress, enjoying the simple soothing feel of cotton, and peed without sitting down on the toilet seat. Reaching for the toilet paper, she saw small writing above it, black marker in a neat round hand, I'll lick you call Ilana, and a phone number with too many digits. Ilana shuddered, flushed, and at the sink washed her hands again, washed them a long time, staring at her white face in the mirror.

She went back to the shop where she bought the dress, but the shop wasn't there. She walked past several windows, back and forth, and the confusion in her grew. Just a few minutes ago, that shop had been there, definitely, and there were two saleswomen, one fat and the other thin and blond, and she had bought a dress which was in the bag in her hand. A store couldn't just disappear like that. She gathered up her courage and asked a few people. No one knew where the shop was. Then she realized she had made a mistake about the level. On her way up the escalator, she looked around at the people wandering with a pleasant hum among the shop windows and felt that she was in a movie. But there was no man in a fine suit waiting for her at the top of the escalator. The fat shop owner, who had just finished talking on the phone, said to her suspiciously, Are you sure you bought that from us, and when Ilana showed her the plastic bag with the name of the shop on both sides in Hebrew and English, the woman said angrily, But you already wore it ma'am, you can't return it now. Ilana explained that she had worn the dress for only ten minutes and that it had been a mistake to buy it in the first place because she was from Haifa, a teacher, and didn't have anyplace to wear such an expensive evening dress. But the woman in black was writing in a notebook and wasn't listening, and the blond saleswoman with the plastic-button eyes just moved her head left and right like a mechanical doll worked by a spring.

Resting her arms on the cool yellow banister, Ilana told herself she'd ask Tami what to do about the dress. Tami would have some solution, maybe she would even offer to buy it from her. Suddenly Ilana felt very tired. She glanced at her watch and couldn't believe it was only twenty to twelve. She had more than five hours before their date. What to do with so much time. She walked slowly, carefully appraising the cafés along the way, to choose the best place to sit. She could sit in a café for half an hour or forty-five minutes. And after she had something to drink and was refreshed, she could think clearly about what to do next. But all the places she passed looked too elegant, and the people were all sitting in couples or groups. Besides, after she had bought such an expensive dress, she couldn't afford to spend a lot more money. She found herself standing in line at a fast-food stand. She bought a hot dog, a big glass of orange juice from a machine, and sat down to eat on a plastic chair next to an artificial plant, her purse and the bag in her lap. She chewed slowly, without appetite and without tasting anything. People passed before her unfocused eyes like tired blotches of color. Three black blotches approached, and Ilana saw three heavyset women. They sat down near her with a sigh and leaned their overstuffed baskets with green leaves sticking out against the legs of the chairs. Stuffing rolls into their mouths, they leaned forward, their thick brown legs twined with blue veins spread so the ketchup wouldn't spill on their dresses. My husband, he takes me to a restaurant every Saturday, after the movies, bragged the one closest to Ilana in a voice choked with hot dog. My husband and I, we only go to his brother and sister-in-law's to eat, grumbled the second one. Mine never goes out, doesn't budge, said the third in a hollow voice. They fell silent a moment and then the first one said, He should rest in peace, he passed away the night before Passover. Ilana stopped chewing and glanced at her in amazement. The woman's hair was dyed red and her feet were puffed out like dough on both sides of her yellow clogs. The second woman, her cheeks furrowed with deep wrinkles, said, Mine, poor man, died the night of Yom Kippur, and she took a huge checkered handkerchief out of her pocket and wiped her nose. Such a good man my husband, whined the third, the thinnest woman, whose nose was beaked so much it almost touched her upper lip, He lent money to everyone. Four, five thousand lire. After he died, blessed be his memory, nobody came to pay it back. My husband lent ten thousand lire, the second one said, raising her voice. Only one man came, paid ten lousy shekels. Oppress the widows and the orphans, the first woman spat, and the other two joined her, Tfoo tfoo tfoo. Then they stood up to go, maneuvered clumsily with their baskets and

finally blended into a single blotch of widowhood, which dwin-
dled to a black dot.

When Ilana shook herself, there was a crushed paper cup in
her hand and a rolled-up napkin stained with ketchup. She threw
them in the trash can, then stood in line again because she
wanted some ice cream. The clock said 11:50. As she was licking
the vanilla-and-raspberry cone, she reminded herself that she
had wanted to see Dizengoff Center, so she decided to go through
the underground passage and walk on the other side for a while.
On the other side, she discovered a fountain whose many streams
of water wriggled on different levels, changing color from pink
to blue to gold according to the lights at the bottom of the pool,
just as in a ballet. Ilana stood smiling at the enchanting sight,
and for a moment she was filled with joy that she was here, in
the miraculous belly of the white beast that seemed to have
everything, and not in school, in the eighth grade composition
class, an especially hard class, where she had to scream sometimes
until she cried, and then in some boring lecture in the gym,
which reeked of mats, dust, rubber, and the sweat of growing
boys, the gym whose ladders and ropes and rings dangling from
the ceiling appeared in her dreams as instruments of torture.

Then she thought of the principal, Abraham, of someone
telling on her and what that would mean tomorrow, but she said
to herself, Don't think about that now, don't spoil your vacation
and your date. The dancing water soared higher and higher in
perfect coordination, and Ilana lifted her eyes and held her breath
until the arcs landed safely with a laughing gurgle. All around
were cafés and shops that sold clothes and shoes and jewelry and
delicacies, exactly as on the other side. She should leave, but
was afraid of the heat outside, here at least it was air-conditioned.
And what would she do outside? It was only five after twelve.

She could look for a present for Tami, a bouquet of flowers. Ilana remembered vaguely that there was a florist's shop on Tami's street. She should buy the flowers there and not carry them around with her, so they wouldn't wilt before five. She began wandering aimlessly along the shops. Thirst grew in her like a rising plant, even though she had just had a big glass of juice and some ice cream. Display windows went by her as a landscape passes a preoccupied traveler. She saw nothing. But her feet kept going, and perhaps she went in circles, because again there was the smell of hotdogs and then the smell of coffee and perfume and American cookies. She didn't know which side of the beast she was on now, the front legs or the hind legs, but her own legs hurt, and her stomach was cramped and her head was spinning and her eyes needed to be shut. They're closing the sea, a forgotten voice giggled through her haze of fatigue, they're closing the sea. Maybe the beach isn't far from here, she thought. She could go and doze there a while on a beach chair in the shade. Enlivened by this idea, she made for one of the heavy glass doors and went out.

A scorching yellow noon panted into her face, as if it had been lying in wait for her. The elderly guard examining handbags at the entrance to the mall gave her directions, pointed to the square, straight, left at Frishman Street, then straight to the beach. At Dizengoff Square, she tried to admire the fountain that spins and plays music, that spits fire and water like a kind of modern dragon, the fountain they'd been talking about so much on television, but her eyes were drawn instead to the old people sitting on the hard cement benches around it. The sun hung over them in the steamy air like a round lemon drop sucking whatever sap they still had left.

On Frishman Street she looked at her watch and was glad to see it was almost one. She heard the familiar ringing of a

school bell and expected to see children running past her in a
group like a blue wave in their school uniforms, but nobody came
out of the open gate, its iron bars reddish brown, and on the
playground there were no boys in sweaty cotton shirts playing
basketball. Ilana stood at the gate, surprised because this school
was exactly like the one where she had spent her youth and now
worked as a teacher: three stories in the shape of an L, dirty
brown walls, the doors green, the window sashes white. On a
sudden impulse she entered and crossed the empty yard, her steps
clicking on the hot asphalt. There weren't even cats sprawled
in the sun or sparrows hopping around to pick up the crumbs
from sandwiches eaten at recess. She climbed the stairs carefully,
trying not to make noise. A few of the doors along the corridor
were closed but most were wide open. She went into one classroom and saw the familiar green board, the formica desktops
scribbled in blue pen with mathematical formulas and irregular
English verbs, the gray iron cabinet in the righthand corner, and
the low wooden platform with the teacher's sloping desk. She
went up on the platform, faced the rows of empty chairs, and
lifted the cover of the desk. A dusty rag was balled up in a corner,
and underneath it lay an English reader. Ilana leafed through
the book until she came to the story Eveline. Her throat tightened as she started reading the story she knew so well from Miss
Moses's English class about the simple girl who fell in love with
a sailor but, in the end, at the last minute, stayed on shore and
didn't go off with him to the happiness he offered. After a few
lines the letters blurred, so she closed the book and put it back
in its place under the rag. The cover of the desk slipped from
her hand with a bang. She went and sat in her assigned seat,
the next to the last on the right, by the window, and read all
the names inside the hearts scratched on the formica top with
a compass point. She looked out, but the green ravine wasn't

there, only gray houses and a large fig tree. She could hear the
voice of Rachel Margolis, who taught her literature in the fifth
and sixth grades and retired after Ilana came back as a teacher,
and now she said to her again, affectionately, Ilana, you're not
paying attention, you're dreaming as usual. Then Professor
Sturm, her math teacher, entered the classroom. He held his
chalk like a conductor's baton and his white pompadour moved
with excitement as he solved, on the blackboard, a long equation
with millions of impossible unknowns. At last, with a flourish
of his baton, he wrote the answer, turned with face beaming to
the rows of unoccupied seats, and made a deep bow. Ilana smiled
but then saw Abraham standing in the doorway. The principal
stabbed her with his tiny eyes, approached, face pale with rage,
and said in his deep voice, emphasizing each word, Why were
you absent from school yesterday. I was sick, whispered Ilana,
her head lowered to the table. He put out his enormous hand,
and said, A note from your parents. I don't have one, whispered
Ilana. You lied, roared the principal, his face red and the veins
in his short neck standing out. Leave! And he pointed to the
door with his thick finger. Ilana quickly left the empty classroom.
On the next door was a sign, Faculty Room. Ilana bent over and
peered through the keyhole. There was no one inside. She turned
the doorknob and entered. In the middle of the room was a long
table made up of a few small tables covered with a dark green
felt cloth, and on it were glass cups with the dregs of tea and
coffee. The ashtrays overflowed with cigarette butts. This was
how their own teachers' room looked after the Wednesday afternoon meeting. The old clock on the wall opposite her said 1:25.
She went to the wall and looked at the photograph of the grad-
uating class. Her eyes wandered over the top row of heads, the
teachers, as if she were trying to find her own face. Suddenly
she heard a rustle behind her. She turned around. In the doorway

stood an old woman in a blue smock and with a flowered kerchief on her head. In one hand she held a mop, in the other, a yellow plastic bucket. Ilana wanted to ask the cleaning woman if today was a vacation in Tel Aviv or if there was a strike, or if school was out early, or if there was some special event, maybe an assembly in the gym, but the old woman straightened up and glared at her with hostile brown eyes, so Ilana left quickly, went down the stairs, ran across the playground and out through the gate, and she went on running along the high bars of the fence until the school, which looked as if some catastrophe had befallen it, was far behind her.

In the distance up ahead, you could now see the sea like a blue kerchief hung out to dry between two white houses. To the left was a movie house named Paris and a big sign announcing the romantic comedy The Lady Eve. The woman in the poster, obviously Lady Eve, was beautiful, with large eyes, black hair, a gleaming evening gown with a long leg stretched forward in a dark nylon stocking and high-heeled shoe. She smiled seductively at the world, at Ha-Yarkon Street in Tel Aviv, and at Ilana, who said to herself, That's a movie I should see. There was a two-o'clock show, in twenty minutes. Ilana bought a ticket at the box office. By the time the movie was over, it would be four, time to start looking for Tami's street, because even though she'd been there once, two and a half years ago, she didn't remember the directions exactly. A shame she didn't have time now to walk on the Esplanade a little and look at the sea, because if she did that, she might be late for the movie, so she stood waiting by the theater. Up ahead was the ice cream man in his white uniform and white visored cap and heavy case that hung from his shoulder by a rifle strap. She could hear his shout, Ice cream chocolate vanilla banana fudgsicles popsicles apricot lemon ice cream. Again she felt thirsty and considered going to the Esplanade to buy a lemon popsicle, but by the time she made up her mind, the ice cream man was too far away and his shout had melted in the heat.

The movie house was cool and comfortable and smelled of Lysol. She glanced around at the rows of seats and discovered she was the first one there. It was ten to two, so she went to the ladies' room and put on new makeup, which was sure to last till five. Then she went back to the theater, still empty, and sat on the right side of the aisle, about in the middle, and put her purse and the bag on the seat to her left. It was now 1:55, and she was afraid there wouldn't be any more people and she'd be the only one watching the movie, alone in the dark theater, and the cashier and the man at the candy counter and the ticket-taker and the projectionist and the usher and the security guard would all have to be here only because of her. People, of course, were working at this hour and wouldn't be going to the movies. Ilana was ashamed. Then she thought that if nobody came in a few minutes, the show would be canceled and her money re-funded, which made her sad, because she didn't want to miss this movie, and also she didn't know what to do for another two hours. At two on the dot, the lights went out and the adver-tisements began, and then Ilana was embarrassed that all this effort to persuade people to buy clothes, bathing suits, cars, cosmetics, diapers, washing machines, refrigerators, and dogfood was directed only at her, who didn't need any of it and didn't have any money either. The door opened, and a shaft of white light invaded the theater. In it, Ilana made out the tall figure of a man. The man closed the door quietly, stood in the aisle surveying the empty rows, and finally sat one seat away from her. He put his James Bond briefcase on the seat in front. What does he want from me, she wondered, but the man smiled at her, and she saw that his smile was open and friendly, his eyes dark and deep-set, his skin fair, his nose small and straight, and his hair brown, thin, and combed back. He turned his face to the screen, and she inhaled the sharp good smell that came from him, familiar and intimate, but where did she know it? Then there was a beer commercial and Ilana recognized her Tami among the people sitting around the wooden table drinking beer and singing. Tami hadn't changed at all, her bouncy curls, blue eyes, lips, and she held a big glass and sang along with everybody, and Ilana felt the song swell and echo in her breast. She wanted to point to the screen and tell the man beside her, See, that's my girlfriend, and this afternoon at five we have a date. After the advertisements, the lights came on and there was a break, and the man looked at her again, attentively now, pensively. Then he got up, tall and thin in jeans and a white shirt with rolled-up sleeves, and left, leaving behind his briefcase and nice smell, but a few minutes later he was back, holding two cans of Coke. No thank you, Ilana whispered, but the white long-fingered hand wasn't withdrawn, so she took the can and whispered, Thanks. It wasn't until she sipped the Coke that she realized how thirsty she was.

Ilana loved the old black-and-white movies that always started with a lion roaring, solemn music, and a lot of names in English which she didn't have time to read. When there was an old movie on television, usually on Wednesday or Friday night, she'd get a chocolate bar with almonds and make a cup of coffee and lie down with a quilt on the living room sofa. The old-fashioned offices, the houses with enormous living rooms and a fire burning in the fireplace, the restaurants and theaters and splendid cars from the forties, it was all a wonderful setting for the beautiful men and women who looked not altogether real and talked easily. Their elegant gestures gave her a special pleasure, and sometimes, when there were emotional partings or

reunions, she'd have to take her glasses off and wipe away her
tears. This movie was set on an expensive yacht and was really
very funny. A woman gambler was using her charms to win the
heart of a rich shy herpetologist. The man beside her put his
head back and laughed, and she felt him looking at her every
now and then in the dark to see if she was enjoying it too. Ilana
sipped the Coke, and the sweetness spread in her stomach. She
tried to concentrate on the movie. How old would the actors be
today if they were still alive, she asked herself and wondered if
they sometimes watched these movies and remembered with sor-
row how they looked when they were young. By now the female
gambler had succeeded in her stratagem and the two of them
were kissing on deck in the moonlight. The man looked at Ilana
for a long time in the pale light of the screen, and she became
extremely embarrassed, her fingers clutching the empty can. The
plot grew complicated. Somebody revealed to the herpetologist
the gambler woman's true identity, and that set off a chain of
errors and misunderstandings, but Ilana couldn't follow it, because the man's glances were getting more serious. She could
almost feel him winding his arm around her and gently stroking
the back of her neck. The two of them finally got married and
went on a honeymoon and the lights came on. Her head down,
Ilana hurriedly gathered up her purse and the bag, and left, but
the man blocked her way in the aisle. He held out his hand and
said, Boris. Ilana, said Ilana, holding out her hand which was
cold from the Coke can. The man shook her hand, then put his
other hand on hers, held it in his palms like a baby bird, smiled
at her with sparkling brown eyes, and said with a soft accent, I
go to café now. Will you like to come to? I can't, said Ilana in
a panic and pulled out her hand, I'm in a hurry, I have a date.
I see, said the man, and sadness blended into his smile. But I
enjoyed seeing movie with you. He turned his back in the white

cotton shirt to her and quickly walked away. She wanted to run after him, to call, Boris, Boris, but her voice didn't obey her and her feet seemed to have fallen asleep. She dropped into the seat, trembling with relief, and looked at her watch. Three-thirty, she said to herself. Just enough time to find Tami's street and buy her flowers.

The usher was sitting at the entrance, an old brown transistor radio pressed to his ear, his glasses steamed from the tea he was dipping cookies in and sucking slowly, with pleasure. Crumbs dropped onto his khaki shirt. How do I get to Balfour Street from here, please, asked Ilana, and he said, What, and put the radio on his lap. She repeated her question, and he answered at length and even drew a tiny map on the back of her ticket stub. She followed his directions to Ben-Yehuda Street and took bus No. 4 down bustling Allenby Street. In a few places, the gray sidewalk squares were being replaced with red bricks, and she thought about the children who now wouldn't be able to play hopping-without-stepping-on-the-cracks. Balfour, said the driver and stopped, and Ilana got out. Here's Tami's street, her heart pounded, and it's only 3:40. She didn't find the florist's shop. In the place she remembered it there was a maternity clothes store. But at the end of the street, in the entrance to one of the houses, she saw an old baby buggy which contained a yellow plastic bucket of bouquets. A small dirty-white dog was tied with a rope to a rusty post, and above the dog was a faded, tattered parasol. As she approached, she saw, behind the buggy, sitting in the doorway of the stairwell, an old man with a wrinkled face, long fingernails, and a gray wool cap on his head. He was half asleep. The flowers looked fresh, so she selected a bouquet of pink and white sweetpeas, went to the old man, and asked, How much. *Finef*, he spat at her. She thrust a creased five-shekel bill into his tiny hand and hurried away. It was four o'clock. She sat on a bench in the shade of a fig tree and without thinking licked the drops of water that sparkled on the colorful petals. On the sidewalk opposite, three children were playing hopscotch. A pair of identical twin girls with black hair, both wearing long denim skirts and yellow stockings, and a boy who was younger. Thin, he wore shorts and a sweater, and his pale face and red curly Orthodox sidelocks bounced in the sunlight under his black satin kippa. Hopping on one foot between the chalk lines, he stumbled and fell. When he got up, his white knees were scratched and his cheeks were flushed with humiliation. He looked around for the kippa which had fallen off his head, but one of the twins got there first, picked it up, shook it off, and the two girls together put it back on his head, using a pin they pulled out of their own hair. They scolded him in Yiddish. The boy, mortified, looked at Ilana, and she was gripped by compassion. A distant radio played, Lushinka, Lushinka, oh where are you, Lushinka, he came back to you, Lushinka, why didn't you wait for him, and Ilana saw herself at fourteen in shorts and pigtails, sitting on the rug next to the big radio in the living room, at dusk on Friday. She hugged her thin knees and let the beautiful Sabbath songs fill her with longing for what she had lost, while pine needles rattled against the window, and the sun, with the last of its strength, turned them into needles of gold.

Yesterday afternoon, at about this same time, she had passed through Carmel Center on her way to her parents' house and met three of her students on the way to their ballet lesson, straight and fresh in pink leotards and hair pulled back. They had smiled at their teacher and said a shy hello, and she longed to stroke their smooth foreheads, and when they walked away, bending their heads toward one another in quiet chatter like three cyclamen plants in a grove, it seemed to her that time had been dozing all these years. Afterward, she went on the path she walked almost every day, crossed in front of Rothschild House, and stopped at the auditorium entrance to read the announcement for the performance of the Stuttgart Ballet next month. She told herself to tell Tami, because even though it had been fourteen or fifteen years since they had stopped dancing, and the old studio on Masada Street was closed, and Valentina Archipova and her husband the spy had disappeared just as suddenly as they appeared more than forty years before, she and Tami still loved the ballet, and she at least didn't miss a single troupe that came to town. She looked out at the paved square between the pine trees next to the old stone building. Once there had been a Rothschild House café here, with round garden tables and chairs with curling white metal backs, and the *Yekkes* of the Carmel, as her mother called them, would come in the afternoon, dressed-up German Jewish women who drank their Viennese coffee and spoke in German as thick as the Sachertorte they ate slowly and politely, spoke about their world before the War until the pines were replaced by the graceless auditorium building and the stone square by cement pavement and the white garden furniture by colored plastic tables and chairs and the Viennese coffee by instant coffee or filter coffee. They still sat here, as in a nature preserve, older but no less grand, and still ate Sachertorte and listened to music and stubbornly stayed alive to remember in German the world of yesterday.

Then Ilana passed the Orly movie house, where on vacations Tami would drag her to matinees of Walt Disney movies, and the wooden seats would squeak and were hard, and the air was filled with excited whispers and the smell of ice cream and Bazooka bubble gum. Near the Orly was a small pastry shop, where Ilana sat with Shmuel on their first date, and afterward they went there often, he always ordering cheesecake and she chocolate cake. Once, after he left, she yearned for him so much on the way home from school that she went in and ordered cheesecake and hot chocolate and found herself writing a poem to him on paper torn from one of her student's notebooks. And here's the shop of the old milliner, where no one was ever seen coming in or going out, and in her display window there were always the same bonnets and high hats trimmed with ribbons and plastic fruit and flowers all covered with dust, and there were wool hats, felt hats, white gauze bridal veils, and even a black top hat in the center dominating all the others. And here's the yarn shop where Ilana came in the winter with her mother, who knitted her a blue sweater for school once every two years, because Ilana grew, and once Ilana bought green yarn here to knit Shmuel a vest for his birthday. And here's Café Par, where on Saturday night, on her way home from Scouts, dozens of dark thin boys congregated, tall in their platform shoes hidden under long black pants that were tight on top and flared at the bottom, and their open colored shirts revealed gold pendants on brown arrogant chests. Their hair was long and full, and they smoked and laughed in loud thick voices, and shouted at her, Hey, Four-eyes, let's have some action, she said through her clenched teeth, Scum, and tried to pass them without grazing their sweaty bodies with her khaki skirt or breathing the smoke of their cigarettes or hearing the laughter of the fat girl who pressed her body in a tight black miniskirt up against one of the boys and rocked on her high heels, her open-mouthed face oozing makeup on his shoulder, and her red-nailed fingers toying with the gold Magen-David on his chest. It was only after Ilana crossed the street that she ran, so they wouldn't think she was afraid, and she ran to Tami's house. Tami had left the Scouts long ago, but she wasn't home because she had gone down to the beach to sing Beatles songs with her current boyfriend, a guitarist who wore dirty jeans scrawled with flowers and phrases about peace and love. He also

tied a leather band around his forehead, and everyone in the
Scouts said he was a hippie and smoked drugs, but Tami said
that was nonsense. Tami seemed shrouded in a secret and was
very pretty in the long embroidered skirt she bought in the Old
City, with a gold chain on her bare ankle and a red ribbon under
her curls. Ilana entered the yard, hoping to find Tami's mother
resting in the garden so she could ask her how her daughter was
and what she had been doing since she came back from America.
But the chaise longue was empty. Ilana stood for a moment
looking at the crumbling boards that were once their treehouse,
and at the big tin barrel filled with sweet rainwater in winter,
brown pine needles floating on the surface and cyclamen bloom-
ing at its base. She remembered how they planned to live in this
yard forever and eat only pinenuts and sorrel, and she thought
that nothing here had changed, everything was only much
smaller. When she got to her parents' house and sat with her
mother at the kitchen table, her mother asked her, as always,
Well, what do you hear from Tami, and Ilana had to tell her
things that she had read in the entertainment section of the
newspaper; Tami was in Israel, busy rehearsing for a new play.
Her mother stopped cutting peapods, sighed, and said, She always
was so wonderful, your girlfriend, and so talented. Invite her
here sometime. Yes, said Ilana, and listened to the five o'clock
news on the radio in the living room.

Ilana forced herself to sit on the bench a while longer. Tami
might be coming home from the theater now and would want
to take a shower. Only when one of the windows above her
opened and a woman's voice blared like an air-raid siren, Moy-
shele, Rokhele, Leahle, and the twins and their little brother
with the red hair flew from the street like three frightened birds,
only then did Ilana stand up, straighten her skirt, bend to see
her face in the mirror of a parked car, quickly smear a little extra

lipstick on her parched cracked lips, and pick up her purse and bag and flowers, which didn't look as fresh as they had an hour ago. She went to find number 37. Lushinka, Lushinka, the song played inside her as she hurried up the steps to the third floor, puffing, and rang the bell. The door didn't open, so Ilana rang again, waited, and rang again. Her heartbeat subsided and her breathing returned to normal. Tami's still at the theater, she said to herself, disappointed, and went downstairs to wait outside. It was 5:10. She sat on the low stone ledge and looked left and right, expecting to see her friend in colorful clothes hurrying to meet her from one end of the street or the other, and then they would hug and kiss with happy shouts and go up to the apartment, and she would tell Tami everything, even about the man in the movie house.

But Tami didn't appear. An occasional car passed, and a breeze began to blow, bringing smells of the sea to the hot streets, waking them from their afternoon slumber. Ilana, terribly thirsty, hoped Tami would come soon so she could ask for a glass of water or juice. I could have gone with him to drink coffee, the thought sliced her heart, and immediately she said to herself, No, I wouldn't have had time. Tami should come any minute. She shut her eyes and buried her face in the pungent flowers, whose petals were beginning to turn brown at the edges. Then she looked at her watch, 5:17, and again up and down the street. A dull dread gnawed at her. Tami would come, of course. She was just a little late. The rehearsal probably ended later than she expected, but she would come. At 5:30, Ilana decided to go up and ring the bell again, on the chance that Tami had been asleep and didn't hear, but this time too the door remained shut, and its Cyclopean eye in the center regarded her, serious and mute. When she came down, she saw a figure in red, running. She tensed and squinted and saw it was a man. He passed, panting, in a jogging suit and sneakers. They had agreed to meet at five. She was sure of that. Tami specifically told her that she was busy in the morning but at five she would be home, and they agreed to meet at five. The watch now said 5:50. The sky turned pale, and the sun was already hanging up its pink scarves and preparing to sink into the sea. A chorus of chirping came from the treetops. A hot gauze of sadness and fatigue collected on the lenses of her glasses, and through it she saw Tami in the distance, and smiled at her, feeling she was in a movie, where the heroine slowly runs toward the hero waiting for her on the beach, in the sunset, and the cameraman deliberately blurs the picture. The familiar figure grew larger as it came toward her, but then Ilana saw it was someone else, someone not beautiful, not at all like Tami. The woman gave her a strange look. Ilana sat on the ledge with her head down and her glasses in her lap. She blew her nose on a used pink Kleenex she found in her purse and tried to calm herself. Something unexpected had come up, yes, something unexpected, and Tami couldn't get hold of her. She decided to wait another fifteen minutes, until 6:30, before she started back to Haifa. The street was wrapped in a pleasant dusk, and the smell of omelets. An obstinate dog barked angrily into the warm air, but then it got tired, and its bark was interspersed with hoarse whining. At 6:30, Ilana could barely see the hands of her watch. She told herself she'd wait a little longer, until 6:45. The flowers were wilted, the pink and white petals covered with ugly dark spots. She threw them into the trash like the used Kleenex. By 6:50, she realized there was no point in waiting. Tami wasn't coming. A heavy fatigue spread over Ilana. All she wanted was to be home, in her bed, and to sleep for a long time. But the house on Bikurim Street was far away. She would have to take a bus to the Central Bus Station in Tel Aviv, and from there it was an hour-and-a-half trip to

Haifa, and from Hadar Ha-Carmel she would have to take a third
bus to Carmel Center, and then there was a twenty-minute walk
to get home. She felt her lips moving. I'm a crazy woman talking
to herself on the street, she thought, trembling, and kept sitting
on the ledge and staring into the darkness. The street lamp above
her came on suddenly with a white light, and the dog burst into
a new fit of barking. Maybe he took it for the moon. Ilanchik,
said a sharp voice, and she lifted her heavy head and said, Tami.

Tami put her cool cheek close to Ilana's and kissed the air.
Have you been here long, she asked, and a torrent of words rolled
out like colored marbles: Tami had completely forgotten that
Ilana was supposed to come, she was half asleep when they talked,
and also she had had a terrible day at the theater. Also, Joel still
wasn't back in Israel and she hated to be alone in the house, so
she sat all afternoon with a girlfriend in a café near here, too
bad Ilana hadn't passed by there. Tami came home only to change
clothes, because she had to go to an opening of an exhibit at
eight. Awfully boring but one has to put in an appearance, you
know how it is, she said sadly and promised to drop Ilana off at
the Central Bus Station on the way, but first they'd go upstairs
and she'd make coffee. So did you have a terrific day in Tel
Aviv, she asked as they turned toward the house. Yes, said Ilana.
Her head hurt and her legs barely carried her up the stairs to the
third floor. Tami dug nervously in her big purse made of colored
patches, pulled out a Donald Duck doll attached to a bunch of
keys, and opened the door. They went into the kitchen, and
Tami put on water, said, Sit here, I'll be right back, and disappeared into the shower. Ilana looked around. The kitchen
hadn't changed except for new appliances from America. She
looked into the living room and recognized the sofa she slept on
two and a half years ago. The phone rang. She didn't know if
she should answer it, but then she heard Tami's voice in Hebrew

and English on the answering machine. She felt glad she was here now, in Tami's house, and not on the other end of the line. The water boiled. She turned off the gas, found the coffee and sugar in the cupboard, took milk out of the refrigerator, and made two cups of coffee. Tami didn't come back, so Ilana went looking and found her in front of the bathroom mirror, wrapped in a black terrycloth robe plucking her eyebrows. Ilana stood behind her friend and saw the bags under her eyes and her faded shriveled lips. She heard herself asking in a strange voice. You remember once, when we were little, we stood in front of the mirror and tried to imagine how we'd look when we were old. No, said Tami. And you said, Ilana went on, that when we were old we'd stand in front of a mirror in the old age home and try to remember how we looked when we were girls. I don't remember, said Tami impatiently, yanking a stubborn hair out of her eyebrow. Then she ran her hand sadly over her wet curls and said, Look, all the gray hair, my head is full of gray. Tami went to listen to the message on the answering machine, called the person, and talked to him for a long time, laughing shrilly. Finally she returned to the kitchen, sat down opposite Ilana, sipped her coffee, twisted her mouth, and said, It's cold. I bought a dress, said Ilana. The words fell out like stones. And it doesn't suit me. I thought maybe you'd want it. Show me, said Tami, her blue eyes lighting up with curiosity. With clammy fingers Ilana opened the plastic bag, displayed the dress. Pretty, said Tami. I would take it but it's too small, I can only wear big dresses these days. Ilana looked at her, uncomprehending, and Tami put her white hands with pink fingernails under the belt of her robe and smiled. Then Ilana understood, and all the blood drained out of her. Fourth month, said Tami proudly. Here, feel. And she stood up, opened her robe, and put Ilana's frozen hand on her warm belly, softly rounded over sheer lace underpants. Ilana began weeping. Her arms tightened as if by themselves around her girlfriend's waist, and her damp face was buried in the fragrant white flesh under the heavy breasts. Stop it, what are you doing, Tami scolded, and tried to extricate herself. But Ilana held on to her and sobbed until she lost her breath. Enough, what's got into you, said Tami, and pulled herself out of Ilana's arms, which dropped helplessly to the sides of the chair. You're tired, said Tami, tying the belt of her robe, and I'm late now. You know I hate to be late. Take the dress, it's pretty. Maybe you'll feel like wearing it sometime. And she folded the dress, put it back in the bag, and laid it next to Ilana's purse. Ilana was still sobbing softly, her eyes on the red and white checks of the tablecloth. She tried to clear her head and understand what was happening. She knew only that she had done something terrible, something she would never be able to repair.

On the way to the Central Bus Station, Tami drove in silence and Ilana looked dully out the window. Just before they got there, she remembered the Stuttgart Ballet and thought of telling Tami, but said nothing. Tami stopped the car. Ilana got out, said good-bye and closed the door. As she started walking, she heard the door open, turned around, and saw Tami slamming it shut again, harder. Then the yellow Beetle went off and disappeared around a corner.

Colored bulbs were now lighted above the cassette stands and falafel stands and reflected in the wet sidewalks. There was a rotten smell. Ilana stood a moment in the middle of the street, trying to decide whether or not to get in the long line that twisted in front of the bus to Haifa. A black minibus stopped next to her with a sharp honk, and the driver stuck his head out the window and asked, Lady, where are you going. Haifa, said Ilana and looked at the sign in the driver's window, which said Hadera. Get in, said the driver and opened the door for her.

But it says Hadera, said Ilana uncertainly, and the driver said, Haifa, Haifa, get in. She sat in back next to an old woman dressed up all in brown and perfumed, who reminded her of the German Jewish women of Carmel. Then a religious man in a long black satin coat got into the minibus and sat next to her. Ilana was surprised, because she knew that Orthodox Jews were forbidden to sit next to women and in front of her, beside the thick-necked black-haired driver, there was another empty seat. The religious man bent forward and muttered impatiently to the driver, Let's go, I'll pay for the empty seat. Ilana glanced at him in amazement, but couldn't see his face, it was hidden under a hat and behind a black beard and metal-framed glasses. The man sat up, took off his coat, and put it on his lap. A musty sour smell rose from his dark suit. She turned her face away, to breathe instead the fragrant perfume of the old woman, but the smell persisted. She paid the driver and shut her eyes, hoping to fall asleep and stay asleep until Haifa, but what if the minibus didn't go to Haifa but only to Hadera? She thought of asking the old woman but was ashamed. The cab's headlights cleared a path in the dark, and Ilana closed her eyes and saw Tami's rounded belly under the black robe, and the mortified face of the little redhaired boy, his knees scratched, and the three empty-eyed widows spitting ketchup as they talked, and the proud cleaning woman in the faculty room of the deserted school, and the young man with disheveled hair and wild eyes who shouted, They're closing the sea, everybody out of the water. Then Ilana saw the face of the man in the movie house watching her over the collar of his white shirt, and she whispered to herself, Boris, and he took her hand in his warm hands and invited her to have coffee with him. They left the theater together and walked to the sea, joining the other strolling couples, and he said something to her in his soft accent, and she laughed aloud, and he laughed with her, until they came to a nice café on the Esplanade. They took seats with a view of the sea and ordered coffee and cake, cheesecake for him and chocolate cake for her, and he stroked her hand which lay on the red and white checked tablecloth and looked into her eyes. She lost track of time, and suddenly the sun was already half in the water, but she didn't say anything and let the man's hand slip under the table and caress her thigh. Something warm was actually on her thigh, she felt, shaking herself out of the daydream. In the darkness, she didn't know if it was the plastic bag stuck to her sweaty leg or the hand of the man next to her, because both his arms, up to the elbow, were covered by the black coat on his lap, and the coat overflowed onto her legs. She shifted in her seat, moved the purse and bag, but there was little room and she still wasn't sure if the man was touching her. She looked at him out of the corner of her eye. He was asleep, or pretending to be asleep. She breathed deeply, trying to ignore the rancid air around him, and waited, rigid, for the next sus- picious movement on his part. A few minutes later, she thought she saw his other hand moving under the coat. She wanted to shout, to say something to the driver, to the other passengers, to ask them to stop the minibus, to let her move to the front seat, but they wouldn't understand, they would look at her as if she were mad, and perhaps her imagination really was running away with her, and she would be mortally offending the religious man. Ilana finally managed to put her purse between her thigh and his, and then he took his hands out from under the coat, stretched, folded them on his chest, and went on sleeping. But, as the cab rolled, every now and then, as if by accident, his fingers would touch her breast. Ilana closed her eyes and prayed that this horrible trip would come to an end, prayed to be in her house and taking a bath, a bad smell she noticed was coming from her too, from her armpits, and after a bath she could get into bed and sleep and not think about anything. The nine o'clock news came on, on the cab radio; disturbances in Judea and Samaria continuing, test-tube triplets born in Bat Yam, hot again tomorrow. Ilana opened her eyes and saw the neon sign Halfway House and realized they had passed Givat Olga, which was right before Hadera. She tensed in Hadera, afraid the driver would stop and she would have to stand in the dark at the intersection and wait for a bus or cab to Haifa. But the minibus passed Hadera and continued on its way, and she relaxed. She tried to return to the movie house in her imagination and start from there again, the walk to the sea, the café, the eyes meeting, the sun setting. Near Zikhron Yaakov, the man in front of her lit a cigarette, and the old woman said in a German accent, Please don't smoke. An argument began, and ended with the driver ordering the man to put out the cigarette. The man opened the window and flicked the burning butt outside, with a string of profanity directed at the driver. Some of the words Ilana knew from her students. Scum, she said to herself, and the driver said calmly to the passenger, Watch your language, mister.

Looking out the window, she was glad to see the sea of Haifa at long last stretching to the horizon, silver in the moonlight like a giant grand piano on whose keyboard the white fingers of a thousand lady pianists were playing. Downtown, the religious man opened his eyes and asked to get out. Ilana thought of the stories she had heard about the whores who walked at night on Independence Road, but she had never seen one. The minibus stopped at Pioneer Street. Ilana got out at the falafel stand and deliberated whether to buy a bottle of soda now or wait until she was home. She went and bought the soda. In the bus to Carmel, she sat down beside the same German woman who had traveled with her from Tel Aviv. The woman turned away, and Ilana again felt how badly she needed a shower. Through a straw

she sucked the sweet liquid all the way to Carmel Center, enjoying the capering lights of her city. They always reminded her
of the treasure chest full of diamond necklaces and precious stones
that Ali Baba discovered in the robbers' cave. At Carmel Center,
she got off and went to throw the empty bottle in the trashcan
by the bulletin board. Under the poster of the Stuttgart Ballet
was an announcement with a black border and in thick black
letters: Rachel Margolis. Ilana stepped closer with dread and read
that the Education Department of the City of Haifa mourned
the passing of Rachel Margolis, devoted teacher, and conveyed
its condolences to the family. Beneath this, in small letters, it
said that the funeral would leave 11:00 A.M. from the cemetery
gate at Carmel Beach tomorrow and buses for the funeral would
leave at 10:30 from the school.

Teacher Rachel's dead, teacher Rachel's dead, her steps
echoed as she went down Bikurim Street. She said to herself,
You're not young anymore, Ilana. She inhaled the night air, the
pines, and was glad that tomorrow at school everyone would be
busy with teacher Rachel's funeral and not remember that Ilana
was absent today, absent for reasons that were not clear, and
had been seen, moreover, on a bus to Tel Aviv.

She opened the door, went in the house. The familiar smell
of old furniture and dusty curtains greeted her, and the smell too
of fried egg from breakfast. She hurried to the bathroom, put
the plug in the tub, adjusted the water to the right heat, and
added a few green drops of fragrant pine bubblebath. Then she
stepped out of her sandals, savored the coolness of the floor on
the soles of her feet, and in one movement pulled the sweaty
flowered dress over her head and pulled off her sweaty underpants
and threw the balled-up clothes into a corner. She took the
scissors from the medicine chest, took her new dress out of the
plastic bag, knelt down on the floor, and began cutting the shiny

fabric, deliberately, thoroughly, back and forth, until the red and black ribbons spun in the room and twisted around her naked body, licking it like tongues. She gathered them up, panting, red in the face, opened the window and threw them as prey to the dark wind of the ravine. The tub filled up. Ilana took off her glasses and her watch, sank into the bubbles, and shut her eyes. On the screen of her eyelids she saw the school playground and herself in a flowered dress. Underneath the dress were baggy blue sweat pants with an elastic waist, and she was running among her students in gym. Then she felt her feet leave the ground, and she took off and flew over the heads of the children, over the windows of the first floor, the second floor, past the principal's window. His eyes widened and mouth fell open, but she flew over power lines and the tops of the pines, red and black ribbons tied to their branches in celebration. Her arms spread out and the wind hit her face and puffed her skirt like a taut sail, and she could see her students lifting their faces to her and watching her flight in wonder. More and more people gathered in the big yard, students and teachers and the school staff, all of them about to go to Rachel Margolis's funeral. Rachel Margolis herself is going to her funeral, and she beckons to Ilana and tells her something that Ilana can't hear, and there's Tami in a pink leotard looking up at her with envy, and a little boy with a pale face and red hair pointing at her and shouting, Look, teacher Ilana is flying, teacher Ilana is flying.